Lessons in Power

A Cambridge Fellows Mystery

Charlie Cochrane

© Charlie Cochrane 2009

Charlie Cochrane has asserted her rights under the Copyright, Design and Patents Act, 1988, to be identified as the author of this work.

First published in 2009 by Linden Bay Romance.

This edition published in 2017 by Lume Books.

Dedication

For my family, who view my writing with a sort of patronising indulgence, and all the friends who've made this series of books a reality.

Table of Contents

Chapter One	9
Chapter Two	21
Chapter Three	29
Chapter Four	39
Chapter Five	49
Chapter Six	66
Chapter Seven	78
Chapter Eight	89
Chapter Nine	99
Chapter Ten	110
Chapter Eleven	119
Chapter Twelve	132
Chapter Thirteen	141
About the Author	149

The ghosts of the past will shape your future. Unless you fight them.

Chapter One

Cambridge, February 1907

"I've been reading a book."

"I remember you saying that once before. We were both stark naked in front of a fire just like this one and by rights should have been making a first consummation of our passion."

Orlando Coppersmith swatted at his friend's head with the first thing that came to hand, which luckily for Jonty Stewart wasn't one of the fire dogs but a bread roll. "It's a constant amazement to me that you've ever shut up long enough for a consummation to take place. *Blether, blether*, if they made it an Olympic event you'd be so certain to be champion that no one else would turn up to oppose you."

"And the point of this conversation was?" Jonty flicked some toast crumbs from his cuff.

"This book concerned the meaning of names and it struck me how apt yours was. Well, it struck me at the time—after the latest bit of tomfoolery I'm not so sure." Orlando, once a potential Olympic frowning champion, smiled happily.

"Handsome, lovely, is that what it means? Statuesque? Desirable?" Jonty chirped away like a little bird, full of the joys of a day which suggested that spring might be just around the corner, if the light filtering into the dining room was any indication.

Orlando grabbed his friend's hands. "Stop it. I'm in deadly earnest. It means 'God has given'. Now if that's not an apt description of you for me then I've no idea what is."

Jonty had the grace to blush. "You'll have to tell Mama. She alleges the choice of Jonathan was all Papa's. *She* wanted to call me James."

"I think I'll start calling you *Godgiven* or some such thing when you're at your most annoying. It might get you to calm down." Orlando buttered his toast with great energy, as if it were his friend's bottom that was getting a whack.

Jonty poked out his tongue, although his lover couldn't be sure whether he was thinking or being insulting. "And what does Orlando mean? Irritating? Insatiable?"

"It's from Roland."

"Well, I'm none the wiser with that."

"Neither was the book, to tell the truth, although it's supposed to be something to do with a famous land. I suspect it means 'he who gains fame throughout the country'."

Jonty turned up his nose. "More likely 'he who spends hours in the bathroom'. Luckily we have two in this place or I'd never be ready in the morning."

In fact there were three bathrooms in their house, but the one in the self-contained annexe—which itself contained Mrs. Ward, their housekeeper—never got taken into the reckoning as they never got to go near it. It was part of the "servant's quarters", as the house agent had referred to them when they'd first enquired about the property, only connected with the rest of the building via a rickety flight of stairs which led to the kitchen.

Not that Mrs. Ward ever complained. Her suite of rooms had been decorated and kitted out beautifully, along with all the rest of the house, prior to the men taking occupation. A sailor's widow in her mid-forties, and with her only son now himself at sea, she'd been recommended to them as a lady who relished the prospect of something to set her abilities to. As the recommendation had come from Ariadne Peters, sister to the Master of St. Bride's college, Jonty and Orlando had paid close attention to it. They didn't want their jobs at the college proving surplus to requirements overnight. Mrs. Ward had a big heart, an open mind and a light touch with pastry, which were the best possible qualifications, and in the fortnight they'd been in residence, the men had no complaints.

Their house, a cottage dating to Tudor times but adorned with later extensions and amendments, had previously belonged to an old lady who'd died. Jonty had spied the property out before Christmas and fallen in love with it. He'd whisked Orlando up there the very evening he agreed to buying a house and the cottage had weaved its magic on him too. They'd bought it before anyone else could, then set to with plans for improvements.

Or, to be accurate, Helena Stewart, Jonty's mother, had descended on her broomstick and taken all the plans for enhancements in hand, as "her lads" were so busy with university business. Soon the Madingley Road was alive with decoration, renovations, plumbing and installation of proper central heating, all without losing an ounce of the property's charm. It was only a matter of weeks before it was habitable and on February the first they took possession.

"Should I carry you over the threshold?" Jonty had been barely able to restrain the bliss in his voice when they'd taken possession. "Or you me? We could even go in, then come back out so we both get a go…" His words had been stopped in the most effective way, by a single, protracted kiss—allowable only as no one else was within a half a mile's sight.

Now it felt as if they'd lived in this house forever. Orlando, whose home for many years had consisted of a set of rooms in St. Bride's in which no one but his students and the Master were allowed—and a chair in the Senior Common Room which no one cared to sit next to—was amazed that his horizons had expanded so far. He kept a room back in college for supervisions, as did Jonty, and their chairs still stood side by side in the SCR, inviolate, but now Orlando had a cottage which he shared in joint names with his lover. He also had second, third, call-them-what-you-would homes in both Sussex and London with the rest of the Stewarts, for whom he was a cross between a fourth son and a favourite son-in-law.

Forsythia Cottage was spacious, affording them each a study to fill with their books, pictures and general clutter. It was well appointed with bedrooms for household and guests, although only one of *their* beds ever seemed to be slept in on any given night. They always took breakfast together, Mrs. Ward serving up ridiculous quantities of bacon and eggs or—as this morning, when talk turned to names— kedgeree, which was spicy and succulent.

"Shall we have Matthew Ainslie up to Bride's for High Table?" Jonty's little nose rose above the newspaper, making him look even more like a small inquisitive mammal than usual.

"Why?" Orlando had managed to avoid having the man visit them through the Michaelmas term, and didn't want things to change now.

"Because we're meeting him at the rugby on Wednesday. It would be terribly rude to just shake his hand after the match, say 'Sorry the university slaughtered Blackheath', and then just leave him there."

It was true; Orlando had to admit that would be shoddy treatment. Even for someone who had once made a pass at him up in the woods. He no longer hated Matthew for past indiscretions, nor wanted to kick him in the seat of his pants, but he was sometimes jealous of the affection Jonty felt for a man they'd only met on holiday. "I suppose so. We can let Miss Peters get her teeth into him if he gets out of hand."

"I'd pay money to see that happen." Jonty drained his cup and poured another. The late Mr. Ward had tasted the excellent coffee supplied in foreign parts and had taught his wife how to make a good brew.

"I suppose in that case we should see about accommodation for him?"

"No need. He's been talking about staying at the University Arms, which seems a better idea than having him here. Then he won't have to listen to your snoring."

"For the one-hundred-and-ninety-third time, I don't snore."

"Don't you?" Jonty stood up and reached over the table for the marmalade, which his lover had appropriated. "Well, some bloke comes in my bed of a night and reverberates. Perhaps it's a farmer driving his pigs to market. Ow!"

Orlando had taken advantage of Jonty's position and landed a hearty slap on his backside. "You'll get another one of those every time you accuse me of snoring."

"Seems a positive incentive to keep on doing it then." Jonty sat down gingerly, although he didn't mind being whacked by his lover—it often led on to something much more pleasant. "I'll ring Matthew at lunchtime, then."

*

"Coppersmith! Orlando Coppersmith!" A chap the size of the great north wall of the Eiger came into view, cutting a lane through the throng of people along the touchline. He grabbed Orlando's hand and pumped it up and down until all the blood flow seemed to cease.

"Morgan." Orlando was pleased to have remembered the name. "I thought you'd have been playing." He jabbed a finger at the pitch, a field as muddy as only Cambridge could produce in early spring.

"Dodgy leg." The man mountain grimaced. "Come to cheer the team on." He offered his hand to Jonty.

"This is Dr. Stewart." Orlando made the introduction with pride. "He played here in about 1876."

"Turn of the century, thank you. I think I may have played against you at some point, Mr. Morgan."

Jonty eyed the man's broken nose and had the vaguest memory that he might just have been responsible. "You beat us then, but I hope we'll make amends today. Ah, please excuse us..."

A hubbub broke out pitchside, which seemed to consist of repeated sayings along the lines of "Matthew, you old dog" or "Jonty Stewart, when are you going to get a decent haircut?" Together with muttered harrumphs from Orlando, which might or might not have been welcoming, this was all accompanied by an outbreak of backslapping, handshaking and general bonhomie. At least two of the three present were pleased at the reunion. For Ainslie, meeting Jonty and Orlando was the one positive thing to have come out of last summer's holiday on Jersey, during which his father had been murdered and these two bright young men had solved the case.

"It's wonderful to be here at last." Ainslie breathed deep of the fresh Cambridge air, so much healthier than the latest London smog.

"All we needed was for you to get here." Jonty's grin couldn't have been wider. "Now we can get a pint of IPA inside ourselves before kick-off. Need the warmth and sustenance."

It proved just as well; the first half of the match was slow, more laboured than they'd hoped, and only the thought of another pint of beer was going to see them through if the second half turned out just as dire.

Orlando went off to find the little boys' room and discussion turned to matters of dangerous binding in the scrum, when Morgan clapped Jonty on the back, sending him sprawling.

The man had been standing close by for the first half, obviously privy to the flow of wit and repartee which passed between the two fellows of Bride's and their guest. "I'd never have thought to see old Coppersmith in such high humour. What happened to him the last few years to make such a change?"

"Oh—" Jonty was, for once, lost for words. Why did people have to ask such bloody awkward questions? Ones to which the wrong answer could lead to two years' hard labour? "Ah, he, um, met a lady who had an extraordinary effect upon him."

"The old dog. I was always convinced he would turn out to be a confirmed bachelor. Any sign of wedding bells?"

"I doubt it. She loves another, you know. Still, he burns a light for her." Jonty was surprised by Orlando slapping his shoulder. He wasn't certain whether his lover had heard what he'd said, although the man would have to be blind not to notice Ainslie's secretive grin.

The game began again, with a bit more swashbuckling spirit on display and, as always seemed to happen, some wag asking whether the referee might benefit from borrowing Stewart's spectacles. A stiff talking-to had no doubt been delivered with the half-time oranges and the end result of two goals all was regarded as being fair.

"Close call, eh?" Ainslie kept his voice low.

"The match or what *he* asked?" Jonty looked sidelong at his guest.

The crowds were wending their way back to colleges, pubs, the train station, wherever they'd come from. Morgan had buttonholed Orlando and was bending his ear up ahead on the path from Grange Road to the river. It was getting dark, the lights of Cambridge appearing like stars in the gloaming.

"It's always the same old story, isn't it? Lies and subterfuge." Ainslie shivered, as did his host. The growing coolness in the air didn't chill them half as much as the thought of the many little deceptions which pervaded their lives.

"I know." They'd reached the river Cam, Orlando still being regaled with rugby tales and looking like he was desperate to escape. "We're off to college to change. Meet us in my set for a sherry before dinner." Jonty shook Ainslie's hand, watched his neat, strong frame make its way along past St. Catherine's, then set off to rescue his lover.

*

"Why did you have to say that?" Orlando's room in St. Bride's provided a sanctuary; here a man could talk freely.

"Say what?" Jonty had forgotten all about the halftime banter. That was forty minutes of rugby, a pleasant walk and a glass of sherry ago.

"About me meeting a lady who loved another. I could hear your voice a mile away. What sort of an impression will they have of me? I thought you didn't approve of lies." Orlando was fuming. Far from making him mellow, the beer had turned him belligerent.

"I don't. Everything I said was true. You met my mama, who is without doubt a lady, and she has had a great effect upon you. And you could never marry her, could you, even if you wanted to?" Jonty looked with regret at the old leather chair by the fire. A nap would be nice but he didn't suppose he'd be allowed one.

"That's being pedantic. It may have been the literal truth but it told a misleading story."

"Well, would you rather I'd said that you'd discovered the delights of my bed, which is the reason why you're so much more confident and worldly wise? Think of the impression that would have caused, Dr. Coppersmith." Jonty knew that he was in the right, and he always made the most of moral superiority.

Orlando was about to argue, then sighed and shook his head. "No, I think this was one occasion when the truth wouldn't have paid." He stared out of the window, musing. "I did wonder why he was being so friendly. He never used to make a point of talking to me."

"You probably used to tell him off for sitting in your chair. Or standing on your bit of the pitch. Now that you're a man of wide social experience, you give off a notable aura of *bon viveur*. Morgan no doubt sees that you've become much more fun to associate with and wishes to become one of your intimates." Jonty began shifting his clothes, or else they'd never make Hall.

"Don't rag me. I was incredibly lonely at times at Oxford. I could have done with a bit more beer and camaraderie then." Orlando hated referring to the loneliness of his pre-Jonty days (or "the blessed times of quiet" as he called them) and if he was doing so now, he must be feeling the emptiness of them.

"Oh, my love. If wishes were horses, then beggars would ride. We can't ever go back and change things can we? If we could, our formative years would all have been quite different."

"I'm sorry." Orlando's loneliness now seemed very small beer compared to the horrors Jonty had been forced to endure at school, experiences it had taken him a great deal of time to recover from. "I didn't mean to—"

"Of course you didn't, whatever it was. Look, we're neither of us the men we were and I daily thank God for it." Jonty, the beer still making his body and spirit glow, felt as though he'd made the wisest pronouncement since the days of Solomon, one which was beyond answer. He was wrong.

"Quite right, too." Orlando fiddled with his cufflinks. "I know you hate it when I speculate about what would have happened if we hadn't met, but I can't help doing it."

"What if we'd met *earlier*? I mean what if we'd been opponents in the Varsity Match? I couldn't have failed to notice you, all gangly legs and unruly curls. I'd have thrown you into touch a few times then we'd have shared a few beers in the bar. It would have been so nice..." There was something about the combination of rugby and beer which made the best of men maudlin.

Orlando snorted. "Well, we could hardly have commenced a relationship out there on the pitch, could we? No, please don't favour that with an answer. It gives you far too much capacity for making obscene jokes about releasing the ball in the tackle."

"I do fantasise sometimes, about what it would have been like to find myself at the bottom of a maul with you on top of me. Shame you mathematicians think it beneath yourselves to rummage up a rugger team—the English mob could organise a fixture and, assuming your old Achilles was up to it..." Jonty drifted off into pleasant reverie. He'd never seen his lover play the beautiful game, so it had become a favourite pastime to try to imagine it.

"Perhaps I can persuade them."

Jonty almost dropped his collar stud. "Do you mean it?"

"Indeed. There's a few chaps new to the university who could well be encouraged to turn out. And I'd enjoy it, too." He smiled, full of mischief.

"Oh yes, Orlando? Being able to take me down in the tackle?"

"And rubbing your little nose into the mud a few times. Can't think of anything better. On a rugby field that is," Orlando added with a grin. "In here, that's another matter..."

But the other matter was never explored, any investigation cut short when Matthew Ainslie knocked on the door in search of his glass of sherry.

High Table was excellent, a corner cut of beef being set off with fiery horseradish, and Yorkshire puddings as light as a feather. Ariadne Peters, whose plain looks were always eclipsed by her sparkling conversation, proved as entertaining as ever, and her brother charmed Ainslie with his intelligent interest in publishing.

They took coffee, cheese and fruit in the Senior Common Room, and when Ainslie accidentally sat in Orlando's chair, the company waited with bated breath for the inevitable explosion of wrath. He astonished them all by sitting in the chair on the other side, letting Jonty take his normal seat. It was a gesture at once simple in its hospitality and profound in its sacrificial nature.

Jonty felt immensely proud of his lover's good grace and resolved that he'd get an adequate reward when they returned home. The conversation meandered on, the wine, quantities of food and warm atmosphere having a soporific effect, so that Orlando soon suggested they take a little air before they all fell asleep. As the three men strolled along, the night air immediately counteracting the feelings of sleepiness, Ainslie spoke.

"Are you free for coffee tomorrow morning at, shall we say, eleven? I didn't want to spoil this evening with business, although tomorrow I'd be grateful if I could—" he seemed to be thinking of the correct term, "—consult you on a professional basis."

Jonty bowed, with only a hint of facetiousness. "That makes us sound conspicuously like Holmes and Watson. I'm available—are you, Dr. Coppersmith?"

Orlando's face illustrated all the frustration he felt. "No, I've college business. And on a Saturday too." He rolled his eyes.

"Then Dr. Stewart will have to take excellent notes, won't he?" Ainslie smiled and strolled off, leaving his friends to find a cab to take them back up the Madingley Road.

Ainslie had found a part of the University Arms where he and his guest could take coffee and talk without being overheard, an important element in his plan, given the potentially delicate nature of the discussion. A University College London man himself, he was enjoying his visit to such a hallowed seat of learning (still hallowed despite Jonty's tales of his less-than-bright students).

Ainslie had ended up with a degree in literature, a taste for port and some interesting connections, which meant he could indulge his inclination towards other men with both discretion and pleasure. A discretion which had temporarily deserted him on Jersey although, thank the Lord, not one which had stood in the way of his friendship with Stewart and his more aloof companion.

He welcomed his guest at eleven on the dot, pouring out a cup of what proved to be an excellent brew. They chatted amiably for a few moments, mainly about the university's prospects in the forthcoming cricket season, then Stewart felt it was time to open his own batting.

"You wanted to talk to us about some sort of case, I take it?"

"Indeed. I remember with extreme gratitude your help on Jersey and I know of your success both before and after it."

Stewart grinned. "You've been reading *The Times*, I suppose, and now you want us to poke our noses into something?"

"That's an unusual way of putting it, but yes." Ainslie was impressed to see Stewart produce, along with his glasses, an elegant notepad and an equally elegant propelling pencil with which he began to make notes. The air of objective authority helped to make a painful situation rather more bearable. "I won't beat about the bush. I have a friend who has been accused of murder. He assures me that he's innocent and I believe that to be the truth. I would like you to see if you can find any evidence to support his case."

"When is this due to come to court?" Stewart's pencil tapped on the page.

"There's likely to be a delay while an important medical witness is recalled from abroad, but we can't be looking at much the other side of Easter." The window gave a faint reflection. Ainslie, catching sight of his face, was shocked at how pale he'd turned.

Stewart was concerned. "And does his own counsel give him any hope?"

Ainslie stared out of the window, at the children playing on Parker's Piece, their delight in running on the grass meaning nothing to his unseeing eyes. "Not very much." All he could see was a face—not his own this time—a handsome young face. One that, time was, had been his greatest delight.

Stewart considered his next question. "If we find evidence that your friend is indeed guilty, what then?"

Ainslie turned, his keen eyes fixing his guest's equally candid ones. "Then he hangs. I'll not have facts suppressed just to bring about the desired result. I want the truth." It hurt to speak every word, yet each had to be said.

Stewart patted his friend's arm. "Good man. Couldn't have taken the job without you having said that.

Now can I have some details? What's your friend's name?"

"Alistair Stafford."

"Should I know him? I'm sure I've heard the name before."

"He's the man who sent that letter to Jersey, detailing my alleged sins to someone who wished to besmirch my reputation." Ainslie watched the children playing yet didn't see them, still registering in his mind's eye a happier time and place.

"Matthew, I don't understand, why should you choose to defend him of all people?"

"We were once lovers, Jonty, very fond and close. We had a misunderstanding, a series of them really, and we couldn't come to any sort of a resolution. We separated under very unsympathetic circumstances—there was a lot of bitterness on his part." Ainslie's gaze remained fixed outside. "Which is why he was keen to give information to my business rival. Spite. Or revenge."

"It's very magnanimous of you to be going to his aid. Was there some rapprochement over the last few months?"

"No, it was his sister who approached me." Ainslie remembered Angela Stafford with fondness—she had never betrayed his friendship. "His mother and father decided to sever ties with him when they discovered where his affections lay. Miss Stafford knew we'd been very close, knew we'd parted, but had no idea, obviously, of Alistair's subsequent betrayal. I didn't enlighten her." He at last brought his gaze back into the room.

"Of course not. Yet you still agreed to help?" Stewart looked so outraged that Ainslie smiled, despite the turmoil in his mind.

"Not there and then, but I agreed to meet him and hear his side of the tale. I was sufficiently convinced—well, to be here now."

Stewart laid down his pencil for a moment. "I feel unworthy to be given such a responsibility. The things we've been involved with in the past haven't been that important, or rather our role within them hasn't. The police would have solved those first two crimes anyway, irrespective of our input. Is there no one else you could ask for help? Someone more competent?"

"There may be, but there's no one I trust half as well as I do you and Dr. Coppersmith. I can be completely candid with you and I'm learning to be so with him. If there's anything to be found, I'm sure that you're the men to find it."

The intellectual detective tried hard not to beam and poised his pencil again. "Can I take a few details?"

"I have some notes here for you—" Ainslie produced a large envelope, "—although I can give you a summary. A man was found dead in his house in Dorking, down in Surrey, the back of his head smashed in with a poker. Alistair was known to have argued violently with him just days before, threatening his life."

"And the man's name?"

"Lord Christopher Jardine." Ainslie almost flinched, so sudden was the change in Stewart's normally good-humoured face. "Did you know him?"

"There was a boy of that name at my school." Stewart was making his face a blank, a mask over it to hide all feeling.

"He'd be a few years older than you."

"Then I did know him." Stewart fiddled with his pencil, some deep emotion welling up, threatening to engulf him.

"I'm sorry." Ainslie's words were sincere but they sounded feeble.
"So am I, Matthew. Sorry I ever made his acquaintance."

Chapter Two

"Got all the gist of the case, Watson?" Orlando had bearded his very own tame lion in its den, or in this instance study. It was one of the nicest rooms in St. Bride's, looking out on honeyed stone and a huge magnolia tree—Ariadne Peters had no doubt had a hand in finding him such a magnificent location.

Jonty managed a smile, but only a wan one. "I've told you before I shan't be Watson. That would make you Holmes and he's an insufferable old sod. You can be Sergeant Cuff, I like him."

"What's wrong?" Orlando knew he wasn't the most perceptive person when it came to other people's feelings, but he was getting pretty efficient at reading his lover's emotions. There was something in the set of the man's shoulders and the tone of his voice that spoke of unhappiness, not a common sentiment for Jonty to display.

"Nothing." Jonty had put up the barriers. He rarely employed them on his lover—today seemed to be a particular, unpleasant exception.

"Don't lie to me. I know you too well by now. Something's eating at you and I'd like to help." Orlando assumed his puppy-eyed expression, knowing it would likely reduce his lover to total compliance.

Jonty slouched in one of the easy chairs in front of the fire. "Pour me a sherry, the decent stuff. One for yourself would be a good idea," he added. "I'm not sure how you're going to react to the story I'm about to tell and a small libation of decent Oloroso usually makes matters easier."

"Tell me all." Orlando handed him a little handsomely cut glass full of a rich-coloured liquid. "Is it to do with what Ainslie had to say today?"

"Matthew's case sounds like a nice juicy one, if you'll pardon the expression. By which I mean it's just the sort of thing we could get our teeth into, although the logistics might prove difficult. You'd be able to go around sniffing for clues and we could ask people questions—real people, rather than dried-up pieces of vellum as you seem to prefer." The sherry was working its wonders on Jonty's spirits.

Orlando tried to look and feel enthusiastic. He relished solving a mystery—if that meant talking to people and being nice to them, then that was the price one had to pay. "And the assignment is?"

"A friend of Matthew's is being tried for murder, probably just after Easter, although the man protests that he's innocent. Matthew believes him and wants us to see what we can do to stop the wrong man going to the gallows."

"So far so good." Orlando, desperate as he was to find out what had upset his lover, knew that as far as Jonty was concerned, discretion was usually the better part of valour. "I can see the logistical problems already, with several more weeks of term and all. I guess it's a case of wise use of weekends and the Easter vac."

"I suspect you're right. We'd need to get all our college work done and dusted before we go to Mama's, so we can spare some time in London—or wherever we're needed—after we've left Sussex. It'll be desperately tight, so every moment will have to count."

"This friend of Ainslie, did you find out much about him?" Inching nearer the cause of Jonty's obvious distress was all that he could do. Slow progress, if progress it was.

"Matthew has kindly written up a detailed résumé of the case; I've skimmed through it so I can give you the gist. The friend's called Alistair Stafford and, believe this or not—and I'm finding it hard to accept—he's the man who was writing all those lies to Sheringham when we were on Jersey."

"'Strewth!" Orlando rolled his eyes.

"'Strewth indeed. I'm not sure I'd have displayed the magnanimity that Matthew has, but he's a Christian soul and has shown true forgiveness."

Jonty began to look so distressed that Orlando moved closer, laying his hand on his lover's arm. "What do the police say happened?" He had to allow his lover to come out with things at his own rate. He'd give him all the time in the world.

"Stafford was arrested a week ago, seven days after the dead man was found. The killing took place in a house in Dorking and the victim's head was pretty well smashed up. You'll have already worked out that means the murder was on February the first, the day we moved in to the cottage. The police know that Alistair had been in the dead man's company two days before his murder and that there'd been words between them concerning treatment of Alistair's sister. Threats were made, specific threats to the victim's life."

"What was the name of this man?" The references to "the victim", "the dead man"—as if Stewart were doing everything to avoid mentioning his identity—were perplexing.

Jonty sighed. "Lord Christopher Jardine." He looked up, held Orlando's gaze. His cornflower blue eyes were full of sadness, a sorrow Orlando only ever saw when Jonty spoke about his time at school. A great light turned itself on in the murky mathematical depths of Orlando's brain.

"Was he one of *those boys*?" There was no need to elaborate any further. Jonty had been badly abused at school—Orlando didn't know all the details, just that he'd been made to endure things, sexual things, unwillingly.

"Yes, Orlando. Christopher Jardine was the first person who ever took me. It should have been you or Richard Marsters or someone who loved me or at least liked me, but it was an evil bastard who just wanted a cheap thrill and enjoyed using a bit of force. He didn't fancy me at all, I'm sure, although I dare say it didn't hurt that I was a pretty boy. It was about power, I suppose."

"I'm so sorry." Orlando put his arms around his friend's shoulders, held him so tight that their hearts were almost pounding one against the other. "I expect you know that already. If there was anything I could do to make that part of your life disappear, I'd do it like a shot."

Kind words and a hug were enough to lift flagging spirits. "Orlando, I love you more than anyone I've ever known—even more than Mama and Papa. For all your faults, none of which I'll elaborate on here, you're a constant source of strength and delight. Of course you'd do that and I'm grateful for it, but Jardine's dead now. And isn't it ironic that we're being asked to establish the identity of his killer?"

Sounds of life came through the windows, ordinary St. Bride's life— untouched, it appeared, by cruelty or moral dilemma. Orlando wished, not for the first time, that life was as simple to solve as his beloved geometry. "That's not strictly true. We're trying to stop the wrong man being hung for the killing."

"Amounts to much the same thing. People like things to be cut and dried—I don't think a judge and jury are going to acquit Stafford unless he has a cast-iron alibi or we can produce the real murderer. This is serious stuff." Jonty rubbed his cheek against his soulmate's.

"Come on, there's more to tell." Orlando laid his long, delicate hand on Jonty's muscular one, troubled to find it clammy and limp.

"Indeed there is. Stafford insists he was at home on his own the night of the killing. He had no one to give him an alibi, and as he only lives at Abinger he wouldn't have had far to travel, not far enough for a juror to have doubts, especially as he keeps a horse and rides it all over the district. He admits to threatening Jardine—says the man was trying to seduce his sister—although he insists this was just his anger talking. He vows he had no intention of actually murdering the man."

"So why is Ainslie so sure he's innocent? Stafford strikes me as a nasty piece of work. We already know he's not above trying to ruin his ex-lover's reputation." Orlando was beginning to feel pangs of guilt at how intriguing he found this case. He treasured the intellectual challenge a mystery gave him, except that this time everything was a little too close to home for comfort.

"Nasty letters are a bit different to smashing in the back of a chap's head with a poker, which is how the police say the thing was done. Stafford promises Matthew he didn't do it, even though he was immensely pleased that his sister's honour was no longer at risk. We have to find out who else might have done the deed." For all that this business touched him profoundly, there was more than a hint of ardour in Jonty's eye, like a hound eager for the chase.

"And would you let that man take Stafford's place in the dock? Wouldn't you feel grateful enough to him to attempt a little massaging of the truth, as we've done before?"

Jonty thought long and, judging by his intense expression, hard. "No, Orlando. Two wrongs, or many more than two if the truth be known, can't make a right. Jardine was a bastard to me, but he wasn't the only one and, while I can't say I'm unhappy that he's dead, I wouldn't want his killer going free just because the victim was such a toerag." He turned his head to land a tender kiss. "Truth above all, it has to be so."

"May I read the summary Ainslie gave you?" Orlando, the growing lump in his throat threatening to betray him, wasn't ready to open up this subject now, not until he'd had time to think.

Jonty nodded, probably—or so Orlando reckoned—reading his mind once more. "Of course, take your time over it. I'm going to find a towel and utilise one of the students' bathrooms. I feel horribly dirty again." He kissed his friend's brow. "I do love you. See you in the usual place before Hall."

Thursday High Table, the day every fellow of St. Bride's was obliged to attend, was a bit subdued compared to the night before, although there was a juicy piece of gossip doing the rounds. Tittle-tattle said the college nurse had spent most of the afternoon moaning to Dr. Peters that he'd not allowed her the privilege of dining with Dr. Stewart's handsome guest the night before and "What was to be done about it, Master?"

Jonty had smirked at the tale, muttering *sotto voce* that he'd hate to see Matthew suffocated in the bosom which ruled the sick bay behind a pinny starched like iron.

He and Orlando were desperate to get away and talk candidly. In the end they had to lie through their teeth, pleading that Jonty had a migraine brewing and needed to return home. Even then, the porter on duty insisted on accompanying them into the street to find a cab, a task he obviously felt was beneath *their* intellectual and social standing.

They reached the cottage, found the pot of coffee which Mrs. Ward had left keeping warm, then settled down on the sofa by the fire.

"What is it about…" Orlando struggled for the right word, had to use one he disliked, "…sex that drives some men? Pandering to the inclinations of the flesh wasn't encouraged in my house. *Mortify your desires*, that was our motto. I got so used to suppressing things that in the end I felt nothing. The first time I had a reawakening of feelings—*down there*, you know—was with you, that day you'd covered my floor with both newspapers and your lovely self. You made rather an attractive rug."

"Like a tiger skin? Or a bearskin?" The pun wasn't lost on Jonty's audience.

"You know, after those fifteen awful months when I was at school I had no inclination towards anything of that nature for years and years. Even just on my own. Wasn't even capable of it—psychologically impotent, clever people would have termed me—not until I had the feelings stirred again. I'm sorry that wasn't with you, as well."

"So am I, as you know." The fire crackled, flames dancing, lighting up their faces. Sadder faces than had been seen in the cottage this last few weeks.

"Jonty, I must know this." Orlando's eyes shone like coals in the reflected firelight. "Are you grateful to whoever murdered Jardine? Wouldn't you want to shake his hand rather than send him to the gallows?"

"I honestly don't know. I can tell myself we're serving justice and that I don't want Matthew's friend unfairly convicted. But when it comes to it—when we have the man or woman in our grasp—I have no idea how I'll react. It's frightening, although it still has to be done and I'll not shirk my duty."

"Good man." Orlando clapped his shoulder. "My Jonty."

"Indeed I am, old thing. Yours forever if you'll have me."

"Do you have any doubt on that score?"

"No. Only the once, when I made such a fool of myself after you lost your memory." Jonty caressed his lover's hands, his long, nimble-fingered, mathematician's hands, as adept with a slide rule or a set of Napier's bones as with a tender touch. "I thought about running away, although I doubt I'd have got further than London. Mama would have dragged me back here and made me apologise to both you and Dr. Peters for being a silly boy." Jonty smiled and kissed his friend's knuckles. "Made for each other, you know. It would take a lot more than a lovers' tiff to split us up."

Sunday morning, Jonty grabbed the last piece of toast out of the rack, then ruffled his lover's hair. "I want to go to the chapel and talk to God, Orlando. I know He sent me you to talk to, for which I am eternally grateful, but this morning it has to be just me and Him."

"I understand." Orlando smiled as he spoke, although he had no idea what his lover meant.

The chapel was warm and inviting. Lumley, the chaplain, insisted it should be made as welcoming as possible—people came to God's house for comfort, not to be put off by cold stone and a forbidding atmosphere. The early communion had finished and Matins was some way ahead, so Jonty could find a comfortable seat and start to think. He said the Our Father, stumbling as always over the as-we-forgive- those-who-trespass-against-us bit, then said a few silent prayers to which only his maker was privy.

His mind raced. Lord Christopher Jardine, first rapist. The Honourable Timothy Taylor, second rapist. Mr. Rhodes (he must have a first name, God would know), agent provocateur, peeping Tom, procurer of unwilling parties. All three of them first-class bastards. Only Jonty, the men themselves, and the Almighty knew exactly what had gone on and who had been involved. Jardine, Taylor, Rhodes—names which Richard Stewart, Jonty's father, would have loved to possess. Names that Mrs. Stewart would have given her fortune to know, which Orlando would have sacrificed his right arm for. Did those parties want the list so they could bring the guilty to justice, or so they could take an appropriate revenge? Jonty shuddered to think.

And now the first abuser was dead, murdered by a vicious series of blows, yet Jonty didn't know how he felt about it. By rights he should be pleased that the swine had got what he deserved, but the hands which did the deed were unknown. It wasn't as if a Stewart or any close friend had committed the act. *Vengeance is mine, saith the Lord*, so perhaps He had used his own agent? But no angel's fiery sword had struck down Jardine—the man had suffered at a pair of all-too-human hands. Part of Jonty felt cheated that his tormentor had never had to face up to his crime, although that had always been his own decision. What point would justice have been if it came at the cost of shame and scandal to the Stewarts?

And I thought I was healed. That was a lie. On bad days, the events still buzzed around Jonty's brain; they sounded in his ears like a heartbeat when he lay down to sleep, screeching in his ears like an alarm when he awoke.

He knew he'd moved on from the broken and bruised Jonty Stewart who'd come to St. Bride's at eighteen being afraid of any contact more intimate than holding hands or the rough and tumble of the rugby pitch. It had taken a long time to reawaken physical desire, but a medical student called Richard Marsters had been patient and kind, full of tenderness. If all he asked was to make love in the dark, then Jonty was happy to oblige, no matter how much he disliked the fact—it had been a small price to pay for getting his life back again.

On those unlit, tender nights there'd been one or two times when Jonty had broken off gasping and crying, imagining he was undergoing his torture again. Richard had always comforted him, even if he couldn't understand. Even if he couldn't return love. He'd seen Jonty as a victim to be tended and looked after, rather than a flesh-and-blood lover to be nurtured, challenged and delighted. At the time it had been enough.

With Orlando things were different. Jonty had been heartbroken at losing his first love, but he hadn't entirely lost his libido, and when at last he found someone who touched his heart again, he'd been able to take the lead, happy to fall into a physical relationship. He wasn't the squirming boy of eighteen—he was a red-blooded male again and in need of a lover. With Orlando he'd been given happiness such as few men are blessed with. Now he could go for a long time without thinking of cold thundery nights at school, although he'd never really forgotten or forgiven.

There remained his distress when it thundered and, while he'd never felt that he was back with his rapists when making love with Orlando, he hadn't been able to put the experiences behind him. When things got "too close", as he called it, like when he was listening to another victim's sad story of his own schoolboy years or when someone had spoken of the sullying of the innocent, he felt acutely aware of memories. Then he could almost think himself back in those cold little rooms, having his innocence wrested from him under extreme duress.

You were never healed, Jonty; he was more than aware of that now. Until he could forgive his predators or confront them—or both—he would find no resolution. He shut his eyes and tried to organise his troubled thoughts into something like a prayer. *I want to get well again, Lord. I know I'm supposed to forgive those who sin against me yet it feels impossible. I know all things are possible for you but I'm only mortal. Please help me.*

Unable to concentrate on his prayers and powerless to find any degree of peace, Jonty opened his eyes. The light playing through the stained glass formed jewelled patterns on the stone flags, bounced off the gleaming brass and illuminated the motes of dust, which danced in the air like Thomas Aquinas's angels.

He must have been transfixed, because the chaplain entered and found him there unmoving, blank, as Orlando had often found him when there were thunderstorms about.

"Dr. Stewart, you're early for Matins." The chaplain touched his shoulder. "Dr. Stewart."

"I'm so sorry." Jonty shook off his stupor, came back to the land of the living again. "I was miles away." *I was years away.* "I'd better go home and meet Dr. Coppersmith, he'll be wondering where on earth I've got to." *Back in that little cold room again.* "We'll be down for evensong. Thank you for being so kind."

"My pleasure, that's what I'm here for. Anytime you need to find some peace and quiet, feel free to come here."

Jonty nodded. "I will." But it was peace and quiet in his own heart that he needed so much and seemed so incapable of finding, even in his Father's house.

Chapter Three

There were only two things Jonty referred to which made Orlando feel uncomfortable, although neither was what had happened at his school. That just made Orlando angry and inclined to fantasise about ice-picks and backs of skulls.

One of the two offensive topics was Richard Marsters. Try as he might, Orlando couldn't rid himself of the jealousy he felt for this man. *He* should have been Jonty's first lover, if there was any fairness in the world. No one else should have been willingly given the privilege of intimacy with that sacred flesh, no other lips or tongue or fingers should have felt, tasted or caressed. But it couldn't be cured so it had to be endured. Under protest.

The other thing was when Jonty referred to how God seemed to speak to him. "Oh, not as a voice in my head, Orlando, although I do get the distinct impression sometimes that He's telling me 'Don't be such a silly sod, Stewart.' The Almighty doesn't mince His words, you know. It's more like a sudden conviction that I must do something, even if I don't want to do it, or the knowledge that something is absolutely right or wrong."

Orlando awaited Jonty's return from Bride's convinced that he'd be made privy to some revelation his friend had received while sitting in the chapel. As it turned out, he was wrong. Jonty seemed pensive when he came back—out of character, but whatever was going on in his noddle stayed there.

They read the papers, enjoyed their lunch, then Jonty suggested that, instead of curling up on the sofa together and snoozing, they should take a brisk and bracing walk. It was dry but overcast and the air was chilling, the layers they'd swathed themselves in proving necessary.

Trying to find early signs of spring proved difficult and conversation waned until Jonty stopped to take a huge breath, watching his exhalation make little clouds in the air as if he were taking a cigar. "I've decided that I can't run away from it anymore."

"I don't know what you're talking about. I've never known you to run from anything. Being too brave by half is your problem."

Jonty smiled and squeezed his lover's arm. "That sounds like me at scrum half, I'll grant you, but I'm talking about what happened at school. I thought if I told myself enough times that I was cured then it would happen, as if repeating something a sufficient amount made it true. Except I can't be cured, not if I still get into a state when there's a storm and certainly not if I can still feel so angry at such a remove. I'm quite happy to find out who killed Jardine and I hope I'll feel no more awkward about it than I have with our other cases. But the resentment's crippling me. I'm angry about Jardine being dead because I don't have the opportunity anymore of beating the living daylights out of him."

Orlando wished they'd stayed at home—not so much because he hated these revelations, it was simple regret they'd not been divulged on the sofa, where he could have held Jonty, petted him and tried to make it better.

"I can't go on getting so wound up over it and now I'm sure about what I have to do. Once we've investigated this case, we're going to find those other two bastards and I'm going to confront them. I have no idea what I'm going to say or do but I have to trust that *He* and you will be there to help me." Jonty smiled, looking quite beatific.

It struck Orlando how much worry had been weighing on his lover, how strained and drawn he'd been looking these last two days. This face, relieved of some of the anxiety, was more like his old self.

"Whatever you feel you must do, I'll be there at your side. Even if we both end up in the dock." Orlando grinned—they both began to laugh, slapping each other's backs in as clear a gesture of love and mutual support as they could risk out on the open road on a Sunday afternoon.

"Do you know, I'm such an idiot. I keep forgetting how lucky I am to have met you and for you to have been daft enough to fall in love with me. We're bound together, Dr. Coppersmith, as surely as if we had taken vows. There should be no secrets any more. I've been a fool not to tell you all."

"If there's more you want to say, Dr. Stewart, might I suggest that we take ourselves home and discuss it at the fireside over a full pot of tea? We'll tell Mrs. Ward to shun the silver service for once."

Mrs. Ward wasn't happy to use Orlando's old brown teapot on a Sunday afternoon, but she succumbed when they agreed to sample her latest batch of butterfly cakes. They snuggled onto the sofa, discarding their shoes and wedging their cold feet under each others' bottoms.

Orlando let the tea and cakes work their magic on his lover's reservations. If he was quiet and sensible, then Jonty would at last pour out all the facts about the days of torment at school. Orlando wanted the names of both perpetrators and the housemaster who had egged them on, so that at the very least he could curse them, swearing at their memory.

"Christopher Jardine was too fond of power and the exercise of it," Jonty began quite unexpectedly, "and Mr. Rhodes—I really don't know his first name, Orlando—saw him as just the sort of arrogant bastard who'd serve his purposes. I suspect that I was just one of a string of boys in St. Vincent house who'd suffered under the auspices of our 'beloved' housemaster. I'm not sure he could have gone without his kicks for too long. Whoever went before me, I don't know, although there was a story that two years after Rhodes came to the school a young lad in St. Vincent's had died in a tragic accident, which someone muttered had been suicide. That was before my time and I've often wondered whether he was another victim. I'm certain there must have been others afterwards, as well, but who those poor souls might be..."

Orlando winced. He'd always assumed, despite one or two hints that Jonty had let drop, that his lover had been the only one to suffer. Now he suspected there were a whole string of young men who needed to heal. He patted Jonty's leg, unable to think of anything constructive to say.

"Anyhow, he goaded Jardine and his pal Timothy Taylor—the Honourable Timothy Taylor, mind you—into performing their nasty little deeds on me, while he watched and got whatever pleasure he could from it."

"How do you know?"

"Because of what *they* said. They made it perfectly clear to me that someone was watching the show and it didn't take long to establish who the peeping Tom was. I think I heard him once, no doubt standing with his hands down his pants giving himself a special thrill every time I pleaded for them not to do it." Jonty studied his waistcoat. He'd done well so far, but his nerve was failing.

Orlando nudged him, opening his arms and beckoning his friend to lounge on him. Jonty didn't need to be asked twice.

"Now we need a plan. To enable us to solve this crime in a short time and at such a distance." Jonty could open his heart no further and, truth to tell, there was little more to come out, sparing the gruesome details. He was already taking refuge in practicalities, as he'd so often taken it in the process of tea making.

"Where do we start? How can we get an idea of what was going on with Jardine?"

Jonty patted his lover's chest. "I'll ring my brother Clarence, he's a member of the same club as milord and he might have an idea. In any case, we'll go down to London for the weekend and get sniffing like a pair of bloodhounds. It'll have to be a hotel as Mama's away—she wouldn't trust us not to lead Papa astray."

"Seems as good a start as any." Orlando rubbed his chin on Jonty's head, a gesture they always found stupidly endearing. "And the rest of today?"

"That's easy. Evensong—I heard you snort, but you'll have to grin and bear it—cheese on toast, and then an early night in bed."

"Early night or *early night*?"

"Depends on how sensible you are in chapel."

"I'll complete the responses like an angel."

"I'll believe that when I hear it…"

Once they'd consumed the last piece of toasted cheese, Jonty had to admit that he did believe it. Orlando had been a saint during evensong, not once frowning or rolling his eyes, even during the sermon, which had in all fairness been one of Lumley's most interesting ones, perhaps because the subject matter— the location and nature of the real Sodom and Gomorrah—had been rather near the knuckle.

They climbed the stairs, in no great hurry, found the fire stoked up in their bedroom, changed into nightshirts against the cold, cleaned their teeth, then slipped into bed, just like a middle-aged married couple.

It was funny, Orlando reflected, how his attitude towards sleeping together had changed so much in a matter of weeks. When they'd first shared a double bed, it had seemed daring in the extreme and the sheer delight of being next to his lover in a state of undress had been enough to make him overexcited. Now that they shared every night, there was no longer the sense of audacity or novelty, although the outcome of any of their romantic encounters remained dazzling.

In fact, Orlando was prepared to swear *that* side of things only got better and better.

This night they lay and read their novels, lighthearted Grossmith for the lover of Shakespeare's sonnets, Doyle with his clinical logic for the mathematically inclined. At a time they seemed to agree on without speaking, they turned out the lights and snuggled into the covers.

Frost was predicted and already the fire was fighting a losing battle against the cold that seeped in through the window. Orlando wound his arms around his lover's body, placing his hand over Jonty's heart, enjoying the feel of its strong and steady beat. His fingers slowly wormed themselves into the gaps between the buttons and twiddled with the scant hairs gracing his lover's muscular chest.

Jonty sighed, wriggling his back into Orlando's stomach. "Sweetheart, would you mind if we didn't go the whole hog tonight? If we just—sort of—played a bit, kissed and cuddled, and the like. As we used to when we were first in love?"

Orlando could only guess at why this unprecedented request had been made, and none of his guesses made him comfortable. When time and opportunity presented, Jonty had never been one to spurn the chance of adventure. "Whatever you want, sweetheart. Your wish, my command and all that."

Jonty giggled. "You do make me feel like I'm a character in some adventure of old. You know the sort of thing, days when knights were bold and maidens were simpering."

"If that's how you want it to be then I'll be your valiant knight. Your Lancelot."

"He rather had a thing for Guinevere, so I'm not sure he's at all a suitable model. Just be yourself, Orlando. It's the thing I love best in all the world."

"Soppy pants. Turn round and let me kiss you."

"Shan't. If you want to be my Sir Orlando you'll have to earn the right to these lips."

Orlando could feel his lover's body shake as he tried to control his laughter. It was one of the most striking things about Jonty and lovemaking—the way he was prone to mirth at the most intimate moments. "And how shall I go about earning it?"

"Be audacious. Be creative."

Orlando needed no second invitation. Creativity no doubt demanded that he couldn't take the easy option of going for the piece of flesh above Jonty's collarbone which, when kissed, sent the man all of a divvy doo-dah, so he would have to find a more novel approach. Unbuttoning Jonty's nightshirt and unpeeling it like the skin of a succulent orange seemed to be a good start—although Orlando reflected that he'd got his fruit analogy wrong. Jonty's skin was more like a firm but ripe peach, soft and covered with a golden fuzz with, in places, just a trace remaining of the tan he'd acquired back in their little cove last summer.

As Orlando made his way down his lover's back, he was struck by the thought that there was one part of Jonty he had never kissed, so he began an immediate assault on it, not just touching it with his lips but licking and tasting, enjoying the unusual feel of the skin.

"You win, you win." Jonty turned over, still laughing. "You've got the right to my lips. And I must say that's the first time anyone has ever made love to my elbow. Really quite an unusual sensation, yet not one I wish to repeat tonight." He kissed his lover with a fire belying what he'd said before. "I do love you, noodle head."

"And I you, fancy pants." Orlando, emboldened by the fierceness of the kisses, began to caress the small of his lover's back, inching his fingers lower until a firm but polite hand removed them.

"Sorry." Jonty's voice sounded small, uncertain, lost. "I just can't be fussed, not tonight."

"I understand." Orlando didn't understand, of course, as much as he tried. The fire dimmed, and the comfort they usually found in each other's arms was for once as paltry as the warmth the hearth gave out.

*

Jonty put the phone down then barged through the door. "The game's afoot."

"What did Clarence have to say? Wasn't he curious about why you were asking?" Orlando laid down his coffee cup and drew his little notebook from a back pocket.

"You underestimate my acting ability, Orlando. I was a picture of innocent remembrance. I'd been at school with Jardine—even my big brother was aware of that. He wasn't in the least surprised that I should be shocked at the murder and want to know what the chaps in town were saying about it. Turns out it was a very fruitful telephone call."

"And? Tell Uncle Orlando all."

Jonty poured himself a cup of coffee then eased himself into a comfy chair. "Jardine was at Platt's— that was his club—staying there for several days, about a week before his death. Nothing unusual about that, but one of Clarence's pals says that milord had one hell of a row the last evening and went home the next day in high dudgeon."

"Did he argue with one of the other members?"

"No. It seems he brought along a guest—they ended up at it hammer and tongs. There may be nothing in it, although it's somewhere to start."

"Can you get someone to take us to the club so we can get the information straight from the horse's mouth?"

"Nothing easier. One of my old colleagues from University College is a member there, too. He'd be more than happy to help to solve the riddle of a fellow clubman's death." Jonty laughed, but his voice was bitter. "He didn't know what Jardine was like, of course. Anyway we can take the train to London on Saturday morning and come back Sunday. I'll ring this chap Troughton and he can take me round to Platt's for lunch the day we arrive."

"Take *you* round? What about me?" Orlando slammed his notepad on the table in a marked manner.

"Got a little commission for you, Orlando, another one of Clarence's gems. According to the official reports, Jardine never left the immediate vicinity of Dorking for the three days leading up to his death, but my brother is prepared to swear that he saw him coming out of Waite's the tailor, on Savile Row, the morning of the day he was murdered. Thought you could start there."

"A Savile Row tailor?"

Jonty wondered whether Orlando would only have been a bit more bothered if he'd suggested a Bermondsey brothel. "The very best. You need to have a title just to look in the window." He grinned at the look of horror which his lover was fighting—a losing battle—to keep from his face.

"Then they won't let me through the door."

"Ah, but they will. Papa is one of their best customers. He can take you there on Saturday morning and get you a new suit on the Stewart account." Jonty revelled in his lover's discomfort. "And *you* can stump up for some new socks. Mrs. Ward says she's embarrassed to put the existing ones out on the line."

*

"Mr. Stewart, always a pleasure to see you." The man's voice and posture carried just the right mixture of deference and familiarity, without being too unctuous. The Stewarts possessed a title of great reputation and antiquity although the present holder refused to use it. No one at Waite's would have been ill-mannered enough to embarrass him by using it.

Richard Stewart gestured magnanimously, taking in the wooden cabinets and glass-fronted displays which exhibited the best that the tailor's had to offer. The place was steeped in fiercely upheld tradition and undoubted quality. "Young Mr. Waite, it is my privilege to bring my custom here."

Orlando was surprised at the *young* part, as the man Mr. Stewart addressed must have been sixty-five at least. Whatever his age, he was glowing with satisfaction at being able to serve such a distinguished customer. "Are we seeking a new jacket for the horse trials? Always prudent to plan ahead."

"Not for me today, Mr. Waite. This is Dr. Coppersmith, from my old college, you know."

Stewart made a sweeping gesture of introduction and Orlando felt like he was expected to curtsey. If he hadn't got such a stalwart companion to hand, he'd have been tempted to bolt, but Mr. Stewart was there to guide and guard him through the harrowing experience. It was almost as reassuring as having Jonty there, the similarity in appearance adding to the sense of support. Richard Stewart was a hand's breadth taller than his son, but of the same sturdy build, and while his hair was more silver than gold, he remained a handsome man. Plenty of female heads had turned as they'd strolled along Piccadilly and not all of them were directed at Orlando.

Waite's gaze appraised him quickly and efficiently. His practiced eye soon noticed that Dr. Coppersmith wore a decent suit, if a little old, although not one of the highest quality. "And what would you require, sir?"

"A new suit. Single breasted. With waistcoat." Orlando spoke with determination, as if he feared being gainsaid. Jonty had warned him how overwhelming an experience a visit to Waite's could be. *We all went there for our first pairs of long trousers. Papa says that Clarence and Sheridan acted like they were in the Headmaster's study, although I found it great fun. Papa had to tell me to be quiet, as I was apparently distracting the man who had the pins and the great big swatches of cloth.* Orlando assumed that Jonty must have had a lot more confidence at thirteen than *he* possessed at twenty-eight.

"And socks." Stewart senior brought his guest's mind back to the matter in hand. "His housekeeper will be most perturbed if we forget those."

Orlando didn't like being measured up; it felt like he was being fitted for a coffin. His unease soon dissipated as Jonty's father decided to open the batting.

"Terrible news about Christopher Jardine."

"Indeed, sir." Young Mr. Waite nodded. "Do you know, his lordship was in here the very morning of the day when he was so brutally attacked? Shocking, quite shocking."

Orlando had a suspicion that part of the blow to Mr. Waite was due to the fact that Jardine's death must have meant good deal of custom lost. He wondered, irreverently, whether the material had already been cut to make whatever garment the man had ordered. "A great sorrow for his lordship's family," he interposed, as a tape measure shot up his inside leg.

"A tragedy, sir. His brother was in here just days later. The funeral..." Waite added, *sotto voce*. They all understood what he meant. "He wanted to take away the half-prepared clothes we'd made for Lord Jardine. Sentimental value. Now, shall we look at some styles?"

The ordeal by inches having finished, they began to peruse pattern books. Orlando had known from the start what he wanted, but it gave them some extra opportunity for questioning as he *ummed* and *ahed* over the exact cut.

"I'd warrant that Jardine was here to pick up some of your excellent hunting jackets." Stewart gave the illusion that he couldn't have cared less what his lordship wanted and was just making conversation while his friend dithered.

"No, Mr. Stewart. Quite the contrary. He ordered some lightweight suits. Now would you like this, Dr. Coppersmith? It's favoured by several of our more academic clients." Mr. Waite indicated a style which must have been worn by Noah when he was up at the University of Ararat.

"That's very distinguished, thank you, but I've decided on this one." Orlando indicated the pattern he'd seen at the start and they began to look at the rich samples of material, which Waite produced by the cartload. Orlando knew exactly which cloth he, or to be more precise, Jonty, wanted, but their plan had been clear in terms of taking his time and maximising every opportunity for gossip.

"It would turn Mrs. Stewart's hair quite white to think that we're in the same place where Lord Jardine had been only hours before he died." Mr. Stewart produced a grave face, one suited to the discussion of death. "Probably the last place in London the victim visited..."

Waite smiled, inclining his head. "Ah, I think not, sir. He told us that he was off to Trimbles for lunch. He was always very talkative and entertaining, his lordship." He cast a sideways glance at someone he no doubt regarded in neither category. "Are we settled, sir?"

Orlando felt that they had sufficient information to be going on with, so he pointed to a rich Welsh woollen mix.

"A very good choice, Dr. Coppersmith." Waite meant it; the swatch was the finest fabric they had in the collection and he was more than impressed that Orlando had selected it. He motioned for the young man who had noted down the measurements to fetch the diary, so that the fitting could be arranged. They settled on a fortnight ahead, with the suit to be ready for picking up when Coppersmith was en route to Sussex for Easter.

"Put this on the Stewart account, please." Mr. Stewart smiled at the surprise, soon masked, on Waite's face. "Dr. Coppersmith is a protégé of my wife's. He was orphaned young and Mrs. Stewart has had him under her wing. She promised him a suit from here when he had his next paper published."

They left the shop, having gained some interesting information and leaving some wondering looks behind them. Stewart beamed. "I feel just like Sherlock Holmes. The Woodville Ward case was entertaining, but that was just a matter of old dry papers. This is much more fun—the game's afoot, eh? And now..." He drew up his shoulders and exhaled with gusto, "Lunch?"

"Indeed. At Trimbles, do you think?" Orlando grinned and they set off.

Chapter Four

There was a spring in Orlando's step. One of the unexpected advantages of having acquired Jonty Stewart as a lover was that he came complete with a family—a family whom Orlando liked and who, miracle of miracles, seemed to like him. He adored Mrs. Stewart much more than he had his own mother, but then Mrs. Coppersmith had never hugged or petted or made him feel secure in the way that Mrs. Stewart did. And the latter lady had only once smacked his bottom.

Now he was beginning to forge the sort of relationship with Mr. Stewart that he'd always wanted to have with his own father—easy yet respectful, serious at times and humorous at others. They took enormous satisfaction in each other's company and, while the thought of having lunch at a ridiculously posh restaurant would normally have made Orlando want to disappear into a hole in the ground, the thought of doing so with Richard Stewart was a most welcome one.

Orlando knew the minute he set eyes on Trimbles that the price would have been out of his league a few months back. Never well off, he'd managed to get by well enough until Jonty had come along and introduced him to all sorts of new delights which had increased his expenditure although his earnings remained much the same. The disparity in income between him and his lover, who'd been well provided for by his grandmother, had been a source of friction between them on many an occasion, until Jonty had been possessed of a brilliant idea.

The old countess, who had been worth a small fortune, had thought that only one of her grandchildren—Jonty—possessed sufficient spark to be given a share of her estate alongside Helena, her only daughter. Among other things, she'd left a boxful of jewellery which was earmarked for his wife, the countess having been oblivious to where her beloved Jontykin's inclinations lay. He'd been in secret consultation with his mother during the summer about whether, morally, he could sell the stuff and set up a trust so that Orlando, who was the nearest thing he'd ever have to a wife, could have a decent income. Mrs. Stewart had talked the matter over with her husband, who'd thought it a splendid plan, especially as it removed the chance that the jewellery might at some point end up in the hands of certain members of his wife's family. People of whom he didn't approve, as they were adulterers and didn't pay their bills on time. Mrs. Stewart had organised it all within a matter of weeks, and Orlando had entered into life at Forsythia Cottage with, for the first time in his life, an income which would allow him to do things at a whim. Like pay for lunch at Trimbles.

The maitre d'hôtel greeted Mr. Stewart with the merest hint of recognition, which was sycophantic compared to the sneers he usually gave people who tried to acquire a table without booking. He found them a suitable place then left them to the ministrations of the headwaiter, who handed them menus and slid napkins onto their laps. "Not our pleasure to see Mrs. Stewart today, sir?"

"I regret to say that she's visiting a sick friend. I will tell her you asked after her." Mr. Stewart smiled, exuding a patrician air.

"Thank you, sir." The waiter turned his attention to Orlando, recognised the tie, then smiled. "A St. Bride's man, sir?"

"Indeed."

"This," said Stewart with a great swell of pride, "is Dr. Coppersmith."

The waiter, Caddick, beamed. "Not *the* Dr. Coppersmith? From the article in *The Times*?"

"The very same."

Caddick bowed to Orlando. "An honour to serve you, sir. I shall take your order whenever you're ready." He scuttled away, full of secret satisfaction.

"What did he mean by *the* Dr. Coppersmith?"

"Don't you remember the article I put in *The Times* about you and Jonty solving the Woodville Ward case? I suspect that in certain circles, the fans of Mr. Holmes for example, you'll have achieved a certain celebrity."

Orlando wasn't sure whether to be pleased or otherwise, and was rather wary when the waiter returned. The man took their order, although he didn't immediately go to despatch it. "I wonder if I might be impertinent as to ask whether you're here in connection with Lord Christopher Jardine?" Caddick cast a knowing look at *the* Dr. Coppersmith.

"We would certainly be interested in hearing anything that you can tell us in that regard. We know that he took luncheon here on the day he was killed," Mr. Stewart interposed, spotting that Orlando was contemplating murder himself.

Caddick nodded, lowering his voice. "Then I'll find the opportunity to come and talk to you at the end of your meal. If there's anything I can help you with, I would be honoured to do so."

Which he was, finding a quiet alcove in the entrance hall where they could speak confidentially; anywhere else would have "not been done".

"Mr. Stewart, Dr. Coppersmith, I know it's true that when someone is murdered, or commits a crime, then people tend to look back and say 'I knew there was something wrong at the time.' Very easy to embroider one's memories, just to impose an idea on them."

"That's correct." Stewart nodded. He had heard such fanciful stuff often before, particularly from his maiden aunt.

"But in this case I did notice something and I said so at the time to the chef. He was most perturbed that Lord Christopher Jardine had sent back his Beef Wellington almost uneaten. I had to reassure him that the dish was excellent, indeed all the other diners had said so, and it was simply his lordship's humour. He'd seemed out of sorts, terribly unsettled all through the meal, and as he left he'd made a particular point, or so it seemed, of finding me to have a word. 'Want to thank you for your excellent service. May not see you again.' I think he had a premonition of his own death." Caddick's face lit up at the thought that he'd been party to such a revelation. "And now I must be back to my tables. Thank you sir, good day."

"A premonition, Orlando?" Richard Stewart raised his eyebrows as the two men descended the marble stairs gracing the front of Trimbles.

"I doubt it." Orlando grinned, alive with the chase. "He was planning to take a trip somewhere and not return for a long time, if at all."

"I agree. No one would be buying lightweight suits at this time of year, otherwise." Mr. Stewart held out his hand for it to be shaken. "I regret that I have to leave you now, to go and attend to some rather tedious business. Give my love to my renegade of a son and tell him you must stay with us when you come up for your fitting."

Orlando nodded. "I'll pass on your orders, although it may take a word from his mother to make him obey."

"Indeed—they're as wilful as each other." Stewart waved for a Hansom cab and strode away purposefully to embark in it.

*

Jonty was waiting, walking to and fro across the foyer of their hotel. "Come on, Dr. Coppersmith, there's not a moment to lose. Been waiting here ages—well, ten minutes at least." There was a nervous energy about him which made his friend uneasy.

"What's up?"

"You'll soon find out—need to get a cab." Jonty almost dragged his lover out of the hotel onto the pavement, frenetically looking up and down the road to catch the eye of a driver, oblivious to the fact it should have been the doorman performing the task.

"What happened at Platt's? I can see that the game's afoot again but I have no idea what it is I'm playing."

"I found out who Jardine argued with. That's the chap we're going to see now, courtesy of the club committee making sure that all guests give their address in the visitors' book."

His efforts to find a Hansom proving fruitful, Jonty bundled Orlando inside the vehicle, giving an address in Chelsea to the driver. He sat looking out the window, rather than the road ahead, the nervous energy that was quite uncharacteristic of him coming to the fore again.

"Does this chap have a name?" Orlando was ill at ease. Something was going on and he wasn't sure he liked it.

The answer took a while to emerge, Jonty's tense breathing almost as loud as the sounds of hooves on the road. "Taylor. Timothy Taylor." Jonty looked his lover straight in the eye, just for a moment, then contemplated the London crowds once more.

"Jonty!" Orlando grabbed his lover's hand, made the man turn towards him. "Taylor? From your school?"

"The very same." Small points of red flared on Jonty's cheeks, fiery indicators of the strain he was under.

"Isn't this being a bit precipitate? Shouldn't we talk it over first?" Rushing headlong into peril—this was wrong, perhaps endangering the whole investigation.

"It's now or never, Orlando. If I have time to think about it then I might never find the courage. *Carpe diem* and all that." The peaks of colour on Jonty's face began to fade now that the truth was all out, being replaced by a steely glint in his cornflower blue eyes.

Orlando nodded, that all made perfect sense. Some tides were made to be taken at the height of the flood. "And did you find out more than the man's name?"

"I did. An old pal of Troughton's was there, one who'd overheard part of the row. It hadn't been very long, or not when they were inside the club. The members soon complained, so the management made Jardine and Taylor leave if they wanted to have such a loud difference of opinion. If the witnesses are to be believed, and I see no need to doubt them, they'd continued their set-to on the pavement."

"Did anyone hear what was said?"

"By the time the voices were raised enough to bother people, it had reached the name-calling stage. Apparently *traitor*, *scoundrel* and *scrub* were some of the more repeatable ones." Jonty looked out at the London streets again, refusing to talk, until the cab drew up outside a rather fine town house in a small exclusive square.

They climbed a short flight of steps then Jonty, taking a huge breath and composing himself, knocked on the door. The sort of butler who obviously regards himself as second in importance only to his master and the king, in that order, opened the portal and eyed the visitors with suspicion.

"We've come to see Mr. Taylor." Jonty fixed the man with his piercing blue gaze, one which reminded Orlando of Mrs. Stewart at her most loud and domineering, a side of him that was, thank goodness, rarely on display.

"Mr. Taylor is not at home, sir." The last word sounded as close to an insult as the butler could manage.

"He may not be 'at home' yet he is at home, I saw him at the window. Please be so good as to tell him that Jonty Stewart is here and that he *will* see me."

There was something in Jonty's tone that was redolent of his dear mama, and even the superior servant had to accede to his will. Jonty and Orlando were left on the doorstep for a few minutes, hearing raised voices inside, before the butler returned to lead them towards the drawing room.

"Mr. Taylor can spare ten minutes." He opened the door and let them into the lion's den.

At least, Orlando had been expecting a lion—some huge man built like a lock forward who could have overpowered Jonty with a single hand. What he met was more like a hyena, a stringy and unsavoury- looking individual who appeared to be built more for cunning than for strength. Even if he hadn't been predisposed to hating the man, Orlando would have taken an instant dislike to him. A peculiar, epicene creature, not at all healthy in appearance, Timothy Taylor was in some odd way a disappointment.

"Mr. Stewart." Taylor rose and held out his hand in an uneasy gesture. The man was clearly worried, as if *his* nemesis had finally caught up with him, rather than the reverse.

Jonty shook the hand perfunctorily. "*Dr.* Stewart. And this is Dr. Coppersmith. We have some questions to ask you."

Taylor's eyes flicked nervously from one to the other. Orlando began to wonder if he thought they'd come to exact a hideous revenge for what he'd done to Jonty. It was an appealing idea, to crush his wretched skull. Or would have been had Taylor been sixteen stone and not such a pathetic specimen of humanity.

"You took dinner with Lord Christopher Jardine at Platt's some days before he was killed. You argued. What was the argument about?" Jonty's voice was hard, unemotional.

Taylor looked shocked, as if this was the last thing he expected Stewart to ask him. He began to relax, re-gather his composure. "That was an entirely private matter and I can't be expected to divulge it."

"You might have to, in a court of law," Orlando chipped in, earning himself a frown from Jonty. He should have realised he was present for moral support—his lover had to be in total charge of this encounter.

"Mr. Taylor, I don't give a fig whether it was a private matter." Jonty resumed the offensive. "You argued and I want to know what the cause was. You will tell me now."

Orlando suddenly saw a strength of character in his friend which was above and beyond any fortitude Jonty had already demonstrated over the last year or so. There was a moral authority about him so imposing it made the man he was interrogating tremble.

"I had a crisis of conscience. I'd done something in the past I was ashamed of and I wanted to make a clean breast of it. His lordship didn't agree with me—I'm afraid we had words over it, to the extent that we were rather ignominiously ejected from the club and made to carry on our disagreement on the pavement. We parted on the worst of terms with the matter unresolved. I didn't meet him again."

"You didn't see fit to visit him in Dorking?"

"Indeed not. It was he who picked the quarrel with me, I had no need to go and plead with him to change his mind." Taylor picked restlessly at his sleeve.

"And this matter, over which you say you had a disagreement, concerned what?"

The silence which descended on the room was broken only by the ticking of the wall clock. Orlando was convinced that he'd counted at least one hundred and eighty-five *tocks* before Taylor spoke.

"You know very well what it concerns, Dr. Stewart. And you have my sincerest apologies, even if I was unable to make Jardine see reason enough to feel remorse over what happened…back then." Taylor raised a handkerchief to his mouth then began to cough. "You will excuse me, I am rather unwell. Is there any more?"

Jonty shook his head. "Not for now. If you've told me the truth then perhaps there will never be more. If not, I'll be back." He turned, an action which Orlando immediately copied. They made their own way out, not waiting for the supercilious butler. They were through the front door, down the steps and halfway along the road before Jonty began to wilt. Orlando grabbed hold of his elbow and, spotting a cab on the other side of the street, hailed it.

"I'd rather get some fresh air." Jonty's pale face certainly looked as if he might benefit from a walk, but Orlando shook his head.

"No arguments. You look like you're about to collapse." He helped Jonty into the carriage, giving their hotel's name to the cabman then taking his rightful place at his lover's side. "And I can't do this while we're walking, out in broad daylight." He slipped his hand into Jonty's, surreptitiously caressing it until a glimmer of a smile appeared on the man's face. "You were magnificent."

"Was I? I felt like a jellyfish. Screwed the old courage up so far, and now I feel absolutely exhausted."

"Then it's as well we get back to the Grosvenor as soon as possible. You can have a bath and I'll have a pot of tea sent up to the room. With treacle tart."

Jonty's wan smile began to increase in wattage. "Treacle tart. My goodness, you know the way to a man's heart, Dr. Coppersmith. A hot soak and tea. You wouldn't consider bringing me a cup while I'm in there, would you?"

"I'll put on my dinner jacket and pretend I'm the waiter if you wish." Orlando was heartened by the banter, always a sign that his friend was regaining his spirits. He dropped his voice—the trapdoor was shut but he suspected cab drivers had ears like bats. "Although I won't play any stupid games like hunt the soap."

Lessons in Power

*

By the time Jonty had been treated to three cups of tea while in the tub and two slices of tart afterwards, his mood was much lightened. He slipped on a red quilted dressing gown and ranged himself along the sofa, holding court. "Do you know, I've been terribly rude. I haven't asked once how you and Papa got on."

Orlando smiled. "Sergeant Cuff, do you mean? He was very keen to be off sleuthing."

"Was any of it successful?"

"Indeed it was. I've a dozen new pairs of socks, all of which will pass muster with Mrs. Ward, and am being fitted for my new suit in a fortnight."

Jonty picked up a cushion and launched it at his friend's head. "You're being deliberately obtuse. What happened vis-à-vis the case? We're short of time, don't forget, and we must make the most of this weekend. Alistair Stafford's solicitor will have men eager to do some legwork, so we need to set them off in the right direction."

"I'm sorry." Orlando adopted his most serious face, although he guessed it no longer fooled his lover. He felt strangely elated, unsettled, and it all dated from their visit to Taylor. He would need to discuss that too, soon. At present he explained all that they'd gleaned at Waite's and Trimbles, offering his and Mr. Stewart's interpretation of it.

"It would fit in with what Taylor said. If he was keen to make a clean breast of things, then Jardine might have felt the need to make a bolt for the continent, rather like all those men did when the Wilde trial came up."

Orlando became even more unsettled. "But that would affect you, wouldn't it? If Taylor made some sort of public admission—and his lordship must have anticipated that the confession would come into general knowledge if he felt the need to flee before it was spoken abroad—it would mean your name being dragged through the mud, too."

Jonty shrugged and looked rueful. "I knew that was a risk I'd be running as soon as we chose to delve into this case. I didn't realise that the wheels might already have been set in motion."

Orlando left his chair and snuggled beside his lover. "I'll stand by you, whatever the outcome."

"I know you will, noodle head. And Mama and Papa. I'm really very lucky. Anyway, does any of this information get us any closer to the real killer?"

"It seems the wrong way round to me. If Taylor was threatening to tell all, then Jardine would have been likely to kill him, not vice versa."

"That's my reaction, too. What's more, if the argument at the club had been overheard and someone fancied chancing their arm at a bit of blackmail, then the same conditions would apply. You wouldn't kill the goose if you could keep the golden eggs in steady supply." Jonty found a stray piece of pastry on his sleeve and consumed it with a sort of schoolboy glee.

"I'd still like to know if Taylor can account for himself on the night the murder occurred. We should put that to Mr. Collingwood and his team of hounds."

"Collingwood is as sound a solicitor as any in the City and he's not afraid of using some slightly less respectable help. He's got some friends of my brother Sheridan off the hook more than once." Jonty smiled, like a child with a secret. "If there's stuff to be found out, he's the man to get to the bottom of it, as long as we can point him in the right direction."

Orlando rubbed his lover's leg. "I was really proud of you today. Couldn't have been at all easy, yet you handled it with such aplomb."

"It turned out a lot easier than I thought, you know. When I saw Taylor, all the thoughts I'd been restraining about beating his head to a pulp just disappeared. He was such a pathetic specimen, I was almost sorry for him."

"Had he changed very much?" Orlando tightened his grip on Jonty's knee.

"He was never built like a barn door, but he was much stronger and athletic back...back then. He seems emaciated now. I believe him when he says he's ill."

"Consumption, do you suppose?"

"Perhaps. Or what my father might describe as *a visitation wrought by the sins of the flesh.*" Jonty grinned again. "Well don't look so puzzled. However will you develop your detecting skills if you don't understand how the world works? I mean a venereal disease, caught off some poor boy he'd hired, I dare say." Jonty may have been sorry for Taylor, but the rancour in his voice remained.

Orlando nodded, trying to appear wise but secretly determined to go off and find a dictionary and delve into the *V* section. Sometime when Jonty wasn't present. "He doesn't frighten you any more?"

"No, Orlando. Best part of fifteen years I've had him as some sort of bogey man in my mind and when I eventually met him, well, I felt rather superior to him. Not just morally, socially as well, if you catch my drift. Look at me, I'm fit and healthy. He's only four years older than I am yet he looked like a man in his late forties. And I have something that I'm sure he's never found." Jonty took his lover's hand. "If I could make what happened at school disappear, never have occurred, but the ultimate cost was losing you, I have no doubt what my decision would be."

Orlando's eyes began to well but, both hands being occupied, he could neither dry nor hide them. "Do you really mean that?"

"Do you doubt me?" Jonty stroked the hands which held his. "No, never. Not my Jonty."

Bustling sounds filtered up from the street, voices, hooves and wheels. Somewhere a peal of bells rang out, London at her lively best. It couldn't spoil the atmosphere within the room, the sense of difficult waters navigated and the safe passage ensured. Orlando shifted closer, placed a gentle kiss on his lover's brow.

"You kiss me so beautifully." Jonty curled into his friend's embrace. "Like you do everything. My Orlando."

At any other time it would have been right and proper for the embraces to go further. Orlando would have breathed into his lover's ear, Jonty would have giggled, and things would have gone to their natural conclusion. Not now, not with this shadow hanging over them. Orlando was sure he could feel a reticence in his friend's touch, a hint of reluctance and regret. The sooner this wretched case was solved, the better.

Chapter Five

Matthew Ainslie watched the contrasting pair of figures meander down the road to the hotel where they were lunching. Tall, dark, saturnine— Orlando's looks only did themselves justice when he smiled, when no one could deny he was handsome. Different in both appearance and attitudes, somehow they formed a perfect pair. Jonty was shorter, stockier, a bright little figure almost dancing along the pavement.

Matthew waved as they approached. "And how have you gentlemen been spending your Sunday morning?"

"Church, a leisurely stroll through Green Park and admiration of the waterfowl." Jonty doffed his hat to the girl at Matthew's side. She was neatly turned out, her checked coat and skirt trimmed with green— young Mr. Waite would have been delighted at its quality. Her hat was topped off with a huge spray of feathers, their artificially bright emerald hue suggesting they'd encountered the dyer's room between bird and milliner. "Miss Stafford, I presume?"

Matthew led them to a small, private room, with a view over the park. The sunshine had raised everyone's spirits and there were more smiles than might be expected from a party gathered in an attempt to save a man's life.

Over an excellent meal they discussed what Stafford's solicitor had come up with, which was very little, given that he had no real leads to follow and no one seemed to be able to give the man the alibi he needed. Jonty and Orlando shared what they'd found out, an enormous amount of information for the small time spent on it.

Matthew was heartened, although he couldn't help feeling, from guarded looks and carefully chosen words, that something was being held back. He'd arranged for Mr. Collingwood to join them later for coffee, the man having a luncheon engagement of his own, and was pleased to have something concrete to offer him.

"We have to establish whether Taylor really was speaking the truth." Jonty laid down his fork and put on his detecting hat. "I'd lay money on his having had further words with his lordship. I can just imagine Jardine going to call on him after he took lunch at Trimbles, trying to resolve things."

"Then wouldn't the murder have occurred in Taylor's house, instead of back in Dorking?" Angela shook her head. "That just seems nonsensical."

"You'd be surprised what sort of things turn up in murder cases. Logic doesn't always play a great part, does it, Dr. Coppersmith?" Jonty turned to his friend, who was deep in thought.

"Hm? Logic? Not necessarily the most useful thing to rely on, the assumption that a killer acted in a totally logical and consistent manner." Orlando was distracted, considering all possibilities. "I was just wondering whether Jardine could have lured Taylor out to Dorking. Perhaps he had the intention of killing *him* and then the plan went horribly wrong."

"His lordship was good at luring people." Angela spoke in a hushed voice, making everyone look at her with interest, but no more on that score was forthcoming at present.

The conversation turned to the cases which the two fellows of St. Bride's had already solved successfully. Matthew was convinced Miss Stafford could tell a great deal more than she was letting on, but he felt certain that his own presence was acting as an inhibitor. Jonty Stewart could charm the birds from the trees—even honey buzzards—so allowing Jonty to work his magic might prove fruitful.

Matthew seized his chance. "Angela, gentlemen, you will excuse me for a moment…" He rose from the table and, while everyone knew where he was going, no one would have been impolite enough to mention it.

No sooner had he disappeared through the door than Miss Stafford grasped her opportunity. "I know that Mr. Ainslie, dear Matthew, has every faith in you and I'm terribly grateful for your efforts, but I fear that they'll all be in vain."

"Why?" Orlando was affronted at the lack of faith in their abilities, their proven track record.

"Because I'm quite sure Alistair is guilty. I know he went out that night, despite what he's told everyone. He wasn't at home when I telephoned him. I would put money on his visiting Jardine and having things out with him." Miss Stafford's eyes were clear and her face determined. No one could doubt she believed her brother to blame. "I'd be immensely grateful if you could find something that would put misgivings into the jury's mind, although I don't believe you'll find another culprit."

"Miss Stafford." Jonty noticed that Orlando's mind was starting to whirr and felt he should occupy their guest so that the wheels of intellect could grind. "Might I be so bold as to ask you why your brother was so cross with Jardine?"

"Because he led me astray. I will tell you this in confidence, although if Matthew returns I must stop—I don't want him to know."

"Dr. Coppersmith, will you go and delay Mr. Ainslie's arrival?"

Orlando's face clouded, as his mind filled with honey buzzards and men taking unnecessary liberties. After a short pause, he agreed. "Perhaps we could go to the bar in search of a cigar, if he smokes the things."

Once Orlando had gone, Miss Stafford continued. "Christopher Jardine paid me many an attention— you could say he quite turned my head. I believed everything he said, which was stupid of me, but I was convinced he wanted to marry me."

"And he didn't?" Jonty found it odd that this girl should be so content to pour out the intimate details of her failed romance to a comparative stranger. Miss Stafford was a pretty enough girl, one who reminded him of his sister Lavinia. Poor Lavinia, whom the astounding Stewart looks had somehow bypassed, leaving her not unattractive, yet no paragon of beauty like her parents or siblings. For all their closeness, Lavinia had never been so forthcoming about her unsuccessful love life.

Miss Stafford sighed. For all her smart-and-modern-young-lady clothes, she suddenly looked like a little girl, lost. "It's the old story. We spent a weekend away together in a hotel. I know you'll think me a complete hussy but I really hadn't done anything like that before. My first time and it wasn't even very nice, although I kept thinking that it would be better when we were married."

Jonty thought of his unfortunate sister and fiddled with his fork.

"But at the end of our stay it became obvious that there wouldn't be any marriage. Well, not between us. I was furious, not just with Christopher but with myself for having been so very naïve. When I told all this to Alistair he went absolutely mad—he found Jardine and had it out with him as soon as he could. Made threats."

"And you believe he carried those threats out?"

"I do. He wanted me to sue Christopher for breach of promise, but the hound had been very careful and left no real evidence of what he'd said." Miss Stafford dabbed her eyes, while Jonty swallowed hard. He knew all about Jardine's ability to cover his tracks. "So the only alternative, if

Alistair didn't want my name dragged through the mud, was to deal with my so-called lover once and for all. Ah, here come our friends." Miss Stafford adroitly changed the subject. "So I'd love to know if Taylor really did have an alibi for that night."

Orlando sat down with a smile. "Don't get Dr. Stewart started on alibis; he doesn't really trust them. If a man said that he was addressing a congress of forty lords spiritual and could produce them all to verify it, my colleague would merely snort and say *so what*?"

"Well of course I would. The man could have got his twin brother to do the speech for him. Strikes me as terribly obvious." Everyone laughed and the tension that pervaded the room was immediately dissipated.

Miss Stafford rose. "You must excuse me, gentlemen, I need to go and call on my aunt." She shook hands all round. "Thank you for the meal and for being so kind. I'll tell Alistair that everything is being done for him."

Orlando watched the girl's departure with such concentration he might have been timing it. The moment they were sure she was out of earshot, he leaned forward. "I'd love to know where she was the night of the murder. Has anyone considered the possibility that she took matters into her own hands?"

"Then why on earth should she want to get help for her brother? Surely there would be the chance that if I employed competent people, her part in things would come to the fore?" Matthew was a straightforward man and the machinations of other people's minds were often a puzzle to him.

"Could be a very clever double bluff if she were absolutely sure she'd covered her tracks." Orlando nodded, as if his view were definitive. "Or it could simply be that she expected us to be incompetent."

"She'd have to be a good actress, though," Jonty chipped in. "She seemed absolutely sincere in everything that she said. There was just the part about putting 'misgivings in the jury's mind' being the best that could be hoped for which might tie in with her being guilty, but that's about all. Now, what time will Mr. Collingwood join us, Matthew?"

"Any moment now, I hope. He can only spare us half an hour, en route from his maiden sister to a rather more affectionate lady, by which I mean a widow living near Regent's Park. He's happy to delay pleasure for business, but only up to a point."

An obliging waiter with a marvellous sense of timing opened the door to their small room and ushered the solicitor in. Collingwood was a fine-looking chap in his fifties, with a military bearing and a sharp eye. He shook hands all round as Matthew made the introductions.

The solicitor listened to all that Orlando and Jonty had to say, his eyes bright and keen. He pinpointed exactly where he could set his own bloodhounds on the trail and seemed surprised when Orlando made such a point of stating that he wanted Angela's movements accounted for, although he noted that down as well. After some discussion about proprieties, it was agreed that he should communicate directly with the Cambridge men and he was allowed to set off to see his piece of Sunday delight.

"I wonder," Matthew began to question his friends as soon as Collingwood had left, "what Angela Stafford can have said to produce such feelings of suspicion in your mind?" He was certain he'd been deliberately delayed in the bar with the offer of a cigar and a discussion on the prospects for the Grand National.

Orlando started a stammering explanation, but was relieved when Jonty smiled and tapped his nose saying, "Client confidentiality, Matthew. It'll all come out if it's relevant."

"I will tell you this." Orlando regained his composure. "When I was young I was brought up to believe that women were just a little lower than the angels, although I never saw a lot of evidence of it from those of my acquaintance. My eyes have been well and truly opened this last year or so—I now regard them as being a most dangerous and vexatious breed. Mrs. Stewart, Miss Peters and our own housekeeper excepted," he added with a grin.

"Oh, I'd figure my mother as deadly and annoying as any of them, Dr. Coppersmith, she just treats you with a ridiculous amount of deference."

"I shall be meeting your mother again soon, Jonty." Matthew had met Helena Stewart before and been impressed. Like Orlando before him, he was also eager to encounter the formidable husband who had tamed this Amazon. "It's something I greatly look forward to."

"It will be her pleasure, too. She's mellowed considerably in her middle years and no longer thumps anyone as regularly as she did in her youth. Just lashes them with her tongue if they step out of line."

Orlando shuddered in remembrance of being caught playing in the snow without his hat on. "I think I'd prefer to be walloped rather than receive another telling-off. Long may I avoid one."

The next two weeks proved frustrating. The fact they could do nothing practical about the Stafford case annoyed both of the fellows a great deal, and St. Bride's English students entertained themselves with a sweepstake on how quickly people could make Dr. Stewart lose his rag. Everyone could see that he wasn't his usual affable self.

He'd had word from Collingwood and his agents, including confirmation that Jardine had seemed to be contemplating flight abroad. More importantly, someone had seen the man have a visitor late on the night he was killed. There was also clear evidence that Timothy Taylor had left his house the day Jardine had died, not getting back until late enough to have been to Dorking, done the foul deed and made his way home. Angela Stafford, however, seemed to have an impeccable alibi, involving not the house of bishops but at least two archdeacons. When Orlando heard this, he merely sniffed, loudly and with emphasis.

Even if their talents couldn't be turned to investigating, they still had plenty to occupy them, as Orlando had been true to his word and organised a rugby match. It was a cold Wednesday afternoon and the crowd, if four dozen people could be called a crowd, thronged the side of the field of play, basking in what little sun there was. The players warming up on the pitch were amazed at how many people had braved the muddied acres of St. Bride's sports field just to witness the team of mathematicians take on the veterans (both in terms of age and experience) of those who studied English.

Although whether what was going on could count as warming up was a moot point. Jonty's team was jogging around the pitch, yet the numerical men were just blowing into their hands and rubbing them together. That was reckoned sufficient for anyone with a bit of spirit, if not appropriate for the effeminate dilettantes who dealt in the Bard or Marlowe. Real men did calculus. And didn't need to stretch.

Word of Dr. Coppersmith's rivalry with Dr. Stewart had spread like wildfire as had the rumour that if either of them came off the pitch without a broken bone it would be little short of miraculous. Jonty had carried on playing since his undergraduate days, with only a short break due to injury, and so wasn't likely to be rusty, unlike Orlando. University gossip reckoned Jonty had been a swashbuckling scrum half in his day and what he'd lost in pace he'd made up for in guile, a cunning which was rumoured to be just the right side of legal at times. But then, as the man himself often said, laws were there to be stretched and explored, were they not?

Miss Peters was there, as everyone expected. She loved rugby and often stomped up and down the pitch shouting on the Bride's boys, much more content than if she were having to be correct and civil with the ladies at church. She understood all the rules—could have refereed the game at a pinch—and the players adored her. They loved to take her off to some establishment after the game to entertain her with white wine. She'd only to smell the wintergreen wafting from the changing room and she was like a greyhound in the slips, ears pricked and waiting for the action to start.

She'd watched Jonty play when he was just eighteen, a boy lacking in self-assurance and a mere shadow of the confident and urbane man he'd become. The thought of seeing how Jonty and Orlando would fare as opponents excited her. She alone in St. Bride's knew the true relationship between the men— would the tackles be entered into as firmly if the beloved was likely to be on the receiving end of them? Her theory was that Jonty would bullet into Orlando without the slightest jot or tittle of a second thought. He'd probably enjoy sending his friend flying into touch and, so long as there were no significant bones broken, then he'd be happy to see a noteworthy number of bruises decorating his darling's limbs or torso. Perhaps there would even be counting of same at Forsythia Cottage, later.

Orlando she was less certain about. Had this match taken place a year or so previously, then the man would have been wary of inflicting any harm upon *his* Dr. Stewart. He'd probably be far less cautious now and might well enjoy the prospect of throwing *someone* on the floor then rubbing his little nose into the dirt before letting him up. Not enough to spoil his looks, naturally; Orlando would be careful on that point.

The English fellows won the toss, which started a rumour that they had a weighted coin as they always seemed to call correctly. The outside half dropped the ball, launched it for the pack to chase and the game was underway. Jonty darted about like a terrier, harrying and tackling, spinning the ball out to set his backs going every time he got possession. The fact that this was a team used to playing together shone from the start—a try was soon scored and converted, the wily Wakefield, who was an expert on the works of Jane Austen, going in under the posts.

Orlando had hardly seen the ball, let alone got his hands on it, and he wasn't impressed. When a pass finally did come his way he was surprised, but with Ariadne Peters in his eye line he couldn't dare spill the ball forward, so he fumbled it into some sort of safe place under his left arm and set off. He'd passed the gain line and spotted a nice little gap between two lumbering forwards—who were no doubt ambling off to where their instinct suggested the next scrum might form—when a cannonball came flying across the field to take him, itself and the ball firmly into touch.

Orlando was winded, the rugby ball flew away, then the cannonball got up with a big grin all over its gob and said, "Sorry, Dr. Coppersmith, don't know my own strength," without meaning a word of it.

By the time Orlando got possession again his side had gone behind even further, but this time he aimed directly for the corner flag, managing to evade all tackles and going over for a virtuoso try. The half ended on an even better note when Orlando managed to tackle the muscular little cannonball and get its face covered in mud, including at least a hundredweight which went up its diminutive nose. As the whistle blew for halftime, honours were even.

When the game recommenced the numerical chaps played with a bit more organisation, getting into their stride and using their brains rather than just their muscles for once. The play drew closer to the English fellows' try line, at which point a loose pass allowed Jonty to intercept the ball in its flight and set off to try to pierce the line of mathematical men. A huge forward (name of Voyce and said to be an expert in the matter of gravitational analysis) lunged at him, took him round the waist and dumped him in a heap over the touchline.

Miss Peters held her breath, not because she feared that Jonty was injured, but because she was near enough to Orlando to see the fearsome look of rage in his eye. The man took off like a train in the direction of the interception, swung the tackler around and squared up to him.

Voyce must have been six foot seven if he was an inch. Orlando wasn't small, but the man towered over him. The look in Orlando's eye would have made even Goliath quail—notwithstanding that Voyce was on his team, there was every possibility of his colleague laying him out with a right hander. The referee (a tiny little scrap of a man who was an expert in botany and who looked as if he made his living impersonating stalks of barley) stepped between them with a firm, "Gentlemen, I don't want to see this. Keep away from one another."

The two players looked shamefaced. Both mumbled a "Yes, sir," and went back to their correct positions for the line out, Jonty's team heartened and amused by the fact that the opposition seemed to be doing half *their* job by sorting each other out. If the left wing and the wing forward were dismissed the field, life would be much easier.

Ariadne Peters eyed the two would-be protagonists with glee—she could see exactly what was going on, if no one else could. Orlando had been happy to slam Jonty onto the ground in the first half. She'd been close enough to see the man deliberately rub his friend's blond hair into a nasty spot of mud so that his usually handsome coiffeur soon resembled a rather dirty haystack. But she would have bet a five-pound note that Orlando regarded this as his prerogative alone, not to be shared with anyone else. If another player dared commit a high or late or otherwise unsuitable tackle on a certain scrum half then he would have Orlando to answer to.

She'd also seen what added to the aggravation. Voyce had deliberately booted Jonty as he lay on the ground while winded, *ergo*, she supposed, he must pay. The game continued apace but Orlando's mind was only half on it. He wanted to avenge his little pal, who'd looked a bit dazed after the tackle although he'd subsequently played off whatever injury he was carrying. Orlando's eye followed Voyce around the pitch, looking for the ideal opportunity—it came when all the circumstances lined up. Voyce at the bottom of a ruck, Orlando in position to rake the ball out, a certain forward's leg exposed, a set of studs on a size-ten boot, a little strafe or two, and not a witness who could say that any of it had been deliberate.

When the final whistle blew, Jonty's team claimed a glorious victory, the mathematical comeback proving too little too late. The teams set off for the communal baths with much clapping and slapping of backs.

When they'd removed all the mud, all concerned repaired to the neutrality of the Bishop's Cope, where the beer flowed and Miss Peters was given a gin and tonic or two to cradle. She mingled with all the players, discoursing knowledgably, and if she lingered with those who had the finest physiques or the handsomest faces, at her age and in her position no one would criticise her.

At last she cornered Orlando, something she'd wanted to do since the game ended, and not in company with his little cannonball-like pal. "A fine match, Dr. Coppersmith, the first of many for your team, I hope."

Orlando beamed. "Most satisfactory, Miss Peters. I'm glad you enjoyed it."

"Oh I did. Though not as much as you, I suspect." Miss Peters had a twinkle in her eye that her brother would have recognised and been wary of.

"Well, I will admit that it was very agreeable to score that try. At least I could equal that drop goal which Dr. Stewart sneaked in."

"Oh, I think that you could easily claim to have outscored him." Orlando's eyes narrowed. "I'm sorry?"

"The referee may not have noticed but I saw what went on in that ruck. Playing at St. George and on your own player too."

Orlando had the grace to blush. "I'm not sure I entirely understand your meaning."

"Of course not, young man." Miss Peters took a sip of her drink. "And don't worry, I won't tell *himself* anything about it. I don't know if he'd be pleased to have a champion or brain you for being a big daft Jessie."

*

Orlando and Jonty arrived at the Stewarts' London home in time for an ample supper and a game of whist, augmented with hugs from Mrs. and back slaps from Mr. Orlando wore his smuggest grin at being with his "family" again—they were spending a weekend in the capital, ostensibly to have the new suit fitted, but with much else to do.

Saturday morning, a visit to Waite's was the first item on the agenda, with Jonty on tenterhooks to see how Orlando would look in a classy suit, the man's clothes up to now having been decent and functional, drab and boring. Even in its rudimentary form, the outfit exceeded all expectation, making Jonty wish he could take a photo to capture the moment, as his father had for him when he'd had his first long trousers. Indeed those very trousers were referred to within thirty seconds of them coming through the door, young Mr. Waite falling on the men and reminding Jonty of all the times he'd been pleased that his establishment had been graced with the family's custom.

As Orlando was poked and prodded with pins, Mr. Waite had gone on to enquire politely after the Stewart family, especially Lavinia's husband, who was also an *occasional*, allowed to do business here on the basis of his father being a bishop.

Jonty let him carry on chatting, having his own clear plan. "I understand from Dr. Coppersmith that an old friend of mine, Lord Christopher Jardine, was in here the day he died. Most distressing for you all." He caught Orlando's eye, wondering if the lie—*old friend*—had been spoken smoothly enough and if he'd given the faintest hint of his true feelings. The slight nod he received in return reassured him.

"Indeed, sir. As we remarked to Mr. Stewart, it was truly dreadful." Waite frowned. "I must admit it's been rather a topic of conversation from his old school friends and fellow members at Platt's. And there has been other, less desirable, interest."

Jonty's ears pricked up. "Not the press, surely?" He knew that such people would be beneath the salt for this establishment and hoped to exploit the shared antipathy to journalists.

"He said he was from the *newspapers*—" Waite managed to make the word sound like it meant sewers, "—although I didn't believe him. He wanted to ask questions but I'd not allow it. Later, I found out he'd been snooping around my staff as well. Most unacceptable."

"I wonder who the scoundrel was?"

Jonty noted the throwaway style of Orlando's question with pleasure. He was getting the hang of this sleuthing business.

"I have no idea, sir, nor do I wish to ascertain an answer. Now, if you would just permit me to take that lapel back a little, I think…" They all admired Orlando's reflection in the full-length mirror.

"Perfect. Mr. Waite, you've excelled yourself." Jonty grinned and set his mind to working out how, now that the tailor had his friend's measurements, he could get three more assorted suits made up without *someone* twigging.

They'd have walked to Timothy Taylor's house, but with time on short commons a cab had to be used and Jonty was left to kick his heels in frustration, urging on the horse by willpower alone. They'd no need to try the strong-arm stuff on the doorstep—Jonty had written to the man in advance to procure an appointment for eleven that morning. Coffee was waiting for them, a thin, evil brew which bore no resemblance to the marvellous stuff Mrs. Ward served up. It was left largely untasted in the cup.

"I want you to tell me where you went to the night that Christopher Jardine was killed." The authority which Jonty felt was evident in his voice.

"I don't have to enlighten you. It was *not* Dorking." Taylor looked superciliously down his nose at them. There was a spark of fight in him, a dash of self-confidence, which hadn't been present at their previous encounter, to such an extent Orlando became convinced he'd been talking to someone about this matter.

"But you had time to go there and back. Ample. If you didn't visit his lordship, then where were you?" Jonty hadn't missed the renewed confidence, although he wasn't going to be put off in the face of it.

"I've said already that I refuse to account to you for all my movements."

"But you would have to tell the police, wouldn't you? And they'd be even more sceptical than I am. You have until Monday. If you haven't sent me word by then about where you were that night, I'll be taking what we know to our friend Inspector Wilson. And Inspector Wilson will make me look like a Sunday school teacher."

"There is one more thing." Orlando reached into his pocket, pleased to see the puzzled reaction on his lover's face. "What can you tell us about this?" He produced a handsome cigarette case, which Jonty would have found familiar.

Taylor took it, examining it all over. "Nothing. As far as I'm aware I've not seen it before; there's no inscription to aid in identifying it." He returned the case.

"The police will find *that* significant, too."

*

"What was all the business with the cigarette case? It looked remarkably like one of Papa's." They were back in a Hansom cab, this time heading for the train to transport themselves south to the subtropical environs of Dorking.

Orlando grinned. "It is. I borrowed it this morning. Can't you guess what I was doing?"

"Acting the goat? Winding Taylor up?" Jonty had no idea what had been going on, not for the first time when it came to the machinations of the Coppersmith mind.

"Partly the latter—it's certainly given him something to think about. More importantly, it's given me a set of his fingerprints and if we do involve the police they might find that useful." Orlando looked so smug he nearly got a slap.

It was the sort of expression which, Jonty surmised, he must habitually wear while teaching his students. He wondered whether it ever provoked any of them into wanting to hit him on the head with a copy of Euclid. "It'll give them yours, too."

"Indeed, but I was very careful only to touch the case around the edges, and now I've wrapped it in a handkerchief." The self-satisfaction had begun to smack of conceit. "Anyway, *my* fingers have never been anywhere they shouldn't have been, have they?"

For some reason Jonty couldn't bring himself to answer that question in such a public place. He stared out of the window, biting his lip and trying not to giggle.

Dorking proved more profitable. They were able to get a clear idea of the accessibility of Jardine's property—close to the railway station, not far from the main roads—and the chances of reaching it unseen (pretty simple, given the amount of shrubbery in the grounds).

They followed the lead Collingwood had given them, knocking at the door of the tiny lodge guarding the end of the drive to the impressive Georgian property Jardine had occupied. They were answered by a jolly, voluble lady who might have been Mrs. Ward's twin sister, given her build and the excellence of the tea and cakes with which she plied her two visitors.

Unfortunately Mrs. Cartwright was less forthcoming with information. It was her husband who'd seen all the activity on the night of the murder and he was now away for a couple of weeks on business. She'd been out, nursing a sick friend, so had missed all the goings on.

She could, however, tell them that the big house had only been rented and that she'd gone up there a few times to help out another friend who had the housekeeping of it. "Not that I want to speak ill of the dead, but I wasn't fond of his lordship. He kept funny hours and enjoyed, well, you'd call it *undesirable company*. There were women who were no better than they should be and men...well, the men don't bear describing." Mrs. Cartwright rolled her eyes.

"I believe you told Mr. Collingwood's agent that there'd been visitors the night his lordship was murdered?" Jonty smiled his most winning smile.

"Yes, sir. At least one. I believe he's being held by the police. Although—" she sniffed contemptuously, "—why Mr. Cartwright hasn't been asked to positively identify him as the man he'd seen, I don't know. I tried to offer information to the local bobby but he sent me off with a flea in my ear for interfering. Well, if the police want any more information now, they'll have to come round cap in hand. It's only right that *they*

Lessons in Power

should do the enquiring, like Mr. Collingwood's man did and *you two nice gentlemen* have done."

The lady beamed, dispensing more tea and more Victoria sponge. She also gave them an address at which they could write to her husband, who'd no doubt, she said, be delighted to furnish them with anything they wanted. Especially, she assured them, if they wrote on college notepaper.

If Jonty was looking forward to a quiet Saturday night dinner with the family, his mother had a surprise in store. It came in the form of a young man, who rapped on the door then shocked the butler as he asked, with a distinct American twang which reached to the drawing room, whether this was the Stewart residence, in which case he was "in the right place and thank the Lord for that".

Rex Prefontaine was about Jonty's age, of a similar colouring and with the same cheeky grin. Orlando wondered whether it was this fortuitous combination of factors which had made Mrs. Stewart invite him, on the strength of a single meeting—or so she informed them as she effected the introductions—to dinner.

Perhaps it was simply her instincts as an experienced hostess which marked Rex out as a potentially delightful guest, something he soon proved to be, witty and urbane without ever dominating the conversation, self-confident without being brash. He was slightly halt in one leg, although none of them would have been rude enough to refer to it.

The darkening, threatening sky made the evening end early, letting Rex return to his hotel before the rain started. He'd not been gone ten minutes before the first crackles of thunder began to make themselves heard away to the south, over the Surrey side of the river.

"Jonathan, whatever is the matter?" Mrs. Stewart had entered the library to find a first edition of *Pride and Prejudice*, which she'd promised to show Orlando. Instead, she found her youngest son standing at the window, transfixed by the lightning as it rent the sky and the thunder shook the panes of glass. "Jonty. Can you hear me?"

"It's all right, Mrs. Stewart." Orlando entered as silently as a panther, realising, as soon as he saw the flashes in the sky, that he'd be needed at his lover's side. The rapidity with which the storm arrived had surprised him and the extra few minutes it had taken to reach the library from the lavatory, where he was attending to a call of nature, had proved crucial. "Don't try to disturb him, let it pass." Orlando reached for Jonty's arm. "It's me, old man, everything's going to be fine."

"What is it?" Mrs. Stewart whispered, her face reflecting the fear that she felt. "I've never seen him like this before."

Orlando felt like he'd been punched. "Never?"

"I wouldn't make light of this, Orlando. Not once. What is it about?"

Orlando could feel the release of tension in his lover's body, a sign that he was coming out of whatever state his mind put him in on these occasions. "I'll tell you later. Can we have some tea? Nice and strong?"

Mrs. Stewart went to ring for the maid while Orlando gently guided his friend over to a deep armchair, murmuring to him all the while. Jonty was quite himself again by the time the brew came. His mother possessed the good sense to have made herself scarce, arriving again simultaneously with the servant who bore the tray.

Jonty pulled himself together sufficiently to give the impression that nothing could possibly have happened, a façade which would have fooled even his dear mama had she not seen him ten minutes previously. He took his tea, pleaded that he needed a good soak and an early night, then took his leave.

Mrs. Stewart waited long enough to ensure her son wouldn't suddenly return in search of a book. "Now tell me what this is all about."

Orlando steeled himself—this wasn't going to be at all pleasant. "It stems from that business at school. The first time *it* happened was a thundery night. Jonty associates it in his mind with storms and seems to shut off from the world, like he's protecting himself from his memories or something."

Mrs. Stewart's naturally rosy cheeks turned ghostly pale. "When he told me about those boys and what they'd done I wanted to go out and strangle them with my bare hands. Or have them pilloried in Trafalgar Square." She began to shake, the emotions she felt written on her face and in her trembling hands. "I call myself a devoutly Christian woman, but finding forgiveness in my heart for those two scoundrels is a real camel-and-the-eye-of-a-needle affair." She breathed deep, trying to look more like her usual, ebullient self. "Has it always happened?"

"As long as I've known him. He doesn't suffer for it—he once used to be a bit distressed, but since..." He stopped abruptly. How could one say to a devoted mother, even one as open-minded as Helena Stewart, *since your son and I became lovers*? Still, it had to be done in some way. "Since we became close, the distress has lessened. He just leaves us and then returns." Orlando studied his fingers.

"Do you know, I should have realised. Whenever storms were in the offing, he took himself off to his room. We thought he was frightened of them and didn't want us to know, him being too proud to admit it. Silly goose." Mrs. Stewart sighed, no longer with the air of a strong and capable woman, just a vulnerable, troubled, loving mother. "Shall I tell him that I know? I might be able to help him if it happens again."

"Better not. I don't think that he would want you to know, not if he hasn't told you already." Orlando felt pained to speak so candidly. He adored this woman, admired her enormously, but he knew that he couldn't entirely share this deepest of secrets yet. "He would regard it as my betraying his trust."

"He would, and that would be heartbreaking." Mrs. Stewart rummaged for her hankie, dabbing at her eyes. "He was such a lovely baby. Perfect, you know. I'm well aware that every parent thinks that of their child but he really was a little smasher and he was so adorable growing up. Fourth child, totally indulged, all he'd known was love and comfort. For him to go out into the world, and that to happen…" The tears were streaming down her face, a visage no less lovely for the wrinkles that all the smiling and laughing over the years had brought.

Orlando dabbed at her tears with his handkerchief. "It's awful, I know. I wish I'd been at that school so I could have done something."

"If I'd known what was going on I'd have stormed down there and thrashed them with my bare hands, the pair of them. And the housemaster with them, because he must have had an inkling. Such a nasty man, I never liked him." Orlando's expressive face gave away that he knew something of that too but his "mother- in-law" didn't choose to pursue it. "I should have known when he came home that first holiday afterwards. The spark had gone. I thought it was just adolescence, especially when he seemed to grow out of it after a few years and seemed happy again. Why did he take so long to tell us?"

Orlando patted her hand, thinking all the time of how he'd never been this close to his own mother. She'd never allowed him to be so close. "He's strong, Mrs. Stewart, but he's not superhuman. He had to find the right time and place. He'd probably been screwing his courage to the sticking place for years." Orlando felt the tears burning his own eyes and employed his already wet linen to clear them. "It's all been stirred up a bit recently. This case that we're looking into; the man who was killed was one of *those boys* and one of the prime suspects is the other. It's all a bit too close for comfort."

Mrs. Stewart fixed him with her watery gaze. "Then give it up, Orlando. I won't have him upset like this. Tell the people involved anything you like, or let me tell them. Better still give me the name of this other suspect and I'll go and see him." Her hands began to shake again and Orlando clasped them. He'd never seen Mrs. Stewart so distressed, so lost for the appropriate word.

"You know I can't do any of those things. Jonty is determined that we see this case through—he feels that it's essential to his recovery to pursue the affair, no matter where it leads. Please don't mention it to him. Let him, let us, deal with things."

"But he's my boy. It's a mother's duty to look after her own." The old fight and spirit was beginning to reassert itself and while Orlando was pleased to see it, he wasn't keen to be in an altercation with his lover's dear mama.

"I appreciate that, but he's mine, too." Their eyes met, like two stags about to vie for ownership of the hinds.

For a moment it seemed like Mrs. Stewart was about to give Orlando a piece of her mind, but she smiled and reached across to kiss his cheek. "Of course he is and I shouldn't interfere. I trust no one with him as well as I trust you. Just look after him, eh?"

"Have you ever known me not to?"

Chapter Six

"Jonty?" Orlando didn't usually knock, making do with barging into his friend's room unannounced, hoping to catch him unawares. On this occasion he not only tapped at the door, but tentatively poked his head around it.

"Hello, sweetheart. Come in and stop making a draught."

Orlando shut the door carefully behind him then wandered across to the huge brass bed, where Jonty lay looking like a schoolboy in his striped pyjamas and with his hair all fluffed up from being washed. It was a sight which filled him with thoughts even more tender than those he'd entered the room with. Orlando ruffled his locks. "Feeling better?"

"Much, thank you. Have you been chin-wagging with Mama?"

Orlando nodded. "A pleasant way to pass the time." He sought refuge in bland words, hoping his friend wouldn't come up with any probing questions just yet.

"And would it be pleasant to pass some time in my bed?" Jonty reached out his hand to finger Orlando's tie. "I have a hankering to lie with my lover which won't be easily gainsaid."

"I think I would like that above all things." Orlando started undressing, as brazen as he'd been the afternoon when he'd got drunk and insisted on using Jonty's bath. That now seemed long ago, an age of great innocence when they knew very little about each other. They knew much more now—hardly anything was kept secret and that only because it didn't really matter in the greater scheme of their lives.

The innocence had now long gone—Orlando couldn't believe what he'd been just a year or so ago. Twenty-seven and a virgin. Twenty-seven and never been kissed. Twenty-seven and likely to remain untouched until he died a dried-up death in a chair in St. Bride's Senior Common Room. Then Jonty Stewart came on the scene and all that had changed. Thank heaven he had.

Orlando wandered through the bathroom which connected their two bedrooms, found his pyjamas, slipped them on, then returned to find Jonty snuggled down, book and reading glasses discarded. Orlando slid between the soft linen sheets, drawing Jonty to him. "I'd hoped it was all over, you know."

"Hmm?"

"This business with the thunder. I always hoped that somehow I could overcome it with my affection for you. 'Perfect love casteth out fear' and all that."

"Well it should do, Orlando, but somehow it's not as easy as it seems. We do have perfect love for each other and I'd regard myself as blessed above all men 'were it not that I have bad dreams'." Jonty shuddered, as if he were shaking off memories as easily as he could shake off his jacket.

"Do you? Nightmares?"

"No, clown." Jonty pinched his lover's backside. "I was quoting your pal Hamlet. It isn't the land of nod, wherever I go when the storms come. I don't feel distressed or see visions, I just visit somewhere else. Very odd."

"I think you go there to protect yourself, in case you remember anything." Orlando smoothed his lover's hair, admiring the golden tones, the hints of auburn the firelight threw up.

"You could well be right. I don't want to remember the gruesome details, thank you." Jonty snuggled onto his lover's chest. "Want to make new memories with you. I think we should somehow wangle it one night, you know, make love while a storm is at its height. That might just get rid of all the trouble. If I could keep *here* for long enough to take an active part."

Orlando held him tighter, kissed his brow. "I suppose I could pinch you or something. Shame there's not been a storm since we got the house—being there would make it easier."

"There'll be plenty in the spring. We just need to plan things. You'll like that, working out your military strategy." Jonty giggled and launched an assault on his lover's collarbone.

"Seems you've got a strategy worked out." Orlando responded by caressing Stewart's back, little, tender movements which always brought contentment to them both.

"Sort of. It's been a long time since we shared the last favours, my love. I've been skittish for too long."

The business with Jardine had become an ever-present menace, as if those who'd committed such outrages on Jonty had somehow found access to his bedroom and were standing gloating, spoiling even the most innocent of pleasures.

Orlando had been frustrated yet endeavoured to understand—he had to be patient, the worst thing to do would be rushing or forcing things. None of this logical reasoning had helped. Now the lowering clouds of unease seemed to have lifted and the sunshine of affection warmed him beyond measure. "If you're sure, I'm ready."

"You always are, Dr. Coppersmith. Since you discovered the delights of the flesh you've become quite a hedonist. Just imagine if I'd taken up that post in Ireland, you'd never have known any of this."

Orlando swallowed hard, hating to be reminded of how close he'd been to not having Jonty by him. "Don't remind me of that. Small turning points, that's what life consists of. One little decision and the whole world changes."

"It does. As it did for us." Jonty reached up to kiss him. "Come on, I want you to lie with me. Been far too long."

Orlando didn't reply. Lips and hands could talk for him, kisses saying *yes* as loudly as tender touches did. Jonty's skin was warmer than expected beneath his boyish pyjamas, and wafts of something lovely, which might have been lavender soap, assailed Orlando's senses as he undid any buttons which had survived his first assault. To feel Jonty's chest against his own, downy skin on smooth, was a necessary part of their lovemaking for him, a sign that they were indeed one, and not meant to be split asunder.

He still wasn't sure how far Jonty wanted to pursue this. There was hesitancy in his touch, some slight tentativeness which didn't usually grace their bed. He gently caressed the small of his lover's back and was pleased to find that, at least for the moment, his hands were allowed to carry on.

Jonty twisted in his lover's arms, using his powerful muscles to turn Orlando, give himself the dominance. He stretched over his lover, a protective canopy against the cold, the world, anything which might disturb them this night. Orlando burrowed into the security, enjoying the unusual sensation of being looked after. He preferred to be the protective one, guarding his most treasured possession, but Ariadne Peters's words had stuck with him. He knew he shouldn't always be the protector.

Tender kisses on the side of his neck made him tingle, firm strokes on his lower back made the sensation spread. However far Jonty wanted to go, he was ready, more than ready. He inched his fingers from the smooth skin of Jonty's lower back down towards their target, a movement which normally brought delighted acquiescence, manoeuvring of body and legs to allow access. Not this time.

"What's wrong?" Orlando spoke into his lover's hair. Jonty had tensed—he was trying to hide it, but Orlando knew.

"I can't. I'm sorry." Jonty pulled away, rolling onto his back and staring at the ceiling.

"Is it this wretched thunder?" Orlando laid a tentative hand on his lover's arm. A protective, comforting gesture, with no hint of desire.

"No. Yes. It's everything." Jonty crossed his arms over his face, shaking off Orlando's hand in the process. "I'm back there, in my mind. A boy of thirteen in a cold room praying for a fire alarm to sound, or anything that would make *it* stop."

"Dear God." Orlando knew this had happened before, but never with him—all he could do was wait for Jonty to come out of the slough of despond.

"Put off the light and go to sleep, sweetheart. I don't think I'll be able to get off for a while."

"Should I stay here? I'll do whatever you think best."

"Please, if you could bear it. I'll be fine, soon. Just tonight…I couldn't do it tonight." Jonty turned, pulling the covers over his head.

"Of course." Orlando didn't attempt to touch his friend. For the moment they were beyond words or contact. There was a chance, more than a chance, that it would be a long time before *doing it* became a viable option again.

Sunday morning meant church and Jonty having to drag a reluctant Orlando there—on such small decisions the world really did depend. At the time, all he could take satisfaction in was there being several members of the royal family present, to whom he was introduced by a smiling and laughing Richard Stewart as the bells rang at the end of the service.

He and Jonty returned to Cambridge before lunch—there were essays to mark and a lecture on *Othello* to revise. Orlando wondered if the inspiration had been recent events. *Very recent events, of an unsuccessful carnal nature.* He desperately hoped that the dunderheads were sufficiently true to their soubriquet not to realise what had supplied Jonty with his new ideas.

On Monday evening a loud rapping on the door of their cottage was followed by a puzzled and perturbed-looking Mrs. Ward poking her head into the lounge to announce that there were two gentlemen to see them, who might just be the police. The initial shock was dispersed when two familiar faces appeared.

Lessons in Power

"Mr. Wilson, Mr. Cohen!" Jonty and Orlando spoke in unison, delighted to see their old friends. Hands were shaken all round and Mrs. Ward sent off to find something small, sweet, and deliciously nourishing, while Orlando played host and poured the sherry.

"To what do we owe this pleasure? If it is going to be a pleasure," Jonty added, his growing sense of unease creating a small knot in his stomach.

"We wondered—" Wilson sipped the excellent amontillado, "—why you had been to see Timothy Taylor." He asked the question innocently enough, although the shrewd light in his eyes showed the police inspector wasn't making small talk.

"Because we've been asked to investigate what a friend believes is a case of wrongful arrest." Orlando knew, they both knew, that there was no point in lying to the constabulary. Although economy with the truth would be judicious.

"And this case is?"

Jonty swallowed, his throat painfully dry, despite the sherry's lubricating effect. "The murder of Lord Christopher Jardine."

There was an interval before Wilson asked his next question. The ticking of the clock sounded louder than it ever had—Jonty was sure the pounding of his heart must have rivalled it. "And your investigations brought you to Taylor?"

"They did indeed, very quickly." Jonty was determined they wouldn't dissemble. Any query would be answered honestly, wherever that led them. The game wasn't just afoot, it was speeding towards the line and he couldn't fail at taking any ball passed to him. "Why do you ask?"

"Because, gentlemen, Timothy Taylor was found murdered yesterday morning and we were told that you'd been to see him on two occasions, the last of which was only Saturday."

If Wilson had been hoping to catch these two men out, to somehow make them show some element of guilt at his revelation, then he wasn't successful. The honest surprise and shock on Jonty and Orlando's faces couldn't have been feigned, not if either of them had been Herbert Beerbohm Tree himself.

"When did he die?" Orlando recovered his composure first.

Jonty hardly heard his question, being brought up with a round turn, as his grandmother would have put it. So Taylor was dead, another one of the triumvirate of bullies struck down by a hand unknown and, by the way in which Sergeant Cohen seemed to be looking at anything in the room except the inhabitants, the police must be wondering if the hand unknown lived in this cottage.

"On Sunday morning at about ten. He'd been fine at breakfast, then had insisted he be left alone until luncheon, which was due at one o'clock. He told the butler that the household were to go to church as they habitually did and that he would see to the door himself should anyone call." Inspector Wilson spoke with his usual note of authority—investigator, judge and jury in one. Not the man to balk at delivering a friend up for justice.

"So he was expecting company?" Orlando had taken out his notepad, was making entries in it— shaky, uncertain entries, or so it appeared to his lover, who could just make out the scrawl.

"He didn't specify that to his staff, but that was their understanding. When the butler came to tell him that his meal was served, he found Taylor with the back of his head staved in."

"Like Jardine." Jonty was astonished at how very small and tremulous his own voice sounded, every word having to be forced out. "He died in the same way."

"Like his lordship, yes. Although I hasten to reassure you that we don't think you have any involvement with his killing." Wilson spoke just a little too hurriedly. Both Jonty and Orlando noticed the discomfort that Cohen was experiencing, his pained expression giving the lie to his superior officer's words. "For one thing you have a superb alibi for the time of the death, although perhaps Dr. Stewart would say that only a guilty man would arrange to be very visibly hobnobbing at church with various members of the royal family when a murder was committed. Please sit down, Dr. Coppersmith, I'm not trying to pick a fight."

Jonty signalled for his friend to be seated, both with a wave of his hand and a particular look in his eye. Getting into fisticuffs with a policeman would hardly further the cause of protesting their innocence. "I find the fact interesting, even though you say we are above suspicion, that you—or I would more properly assume one of your colleagues in London—checked exactly where we were on Sunday morning. Or is it the case that we only lost the cloud of doubt once you'd established that we couldn't have been there to do the deed?"

Jonty knew he was illogical to feel so angry, because the police were going through the same thought processes which he and Orlando would have employed if the roles had been reversed. *Yet it's not the fact that we've been checked on that riles me. It's knowing Orlando nearly didn't attend service the previous morning. If the silly sod had stayed at home, he'd have been under the gravest suspicion now.* A quick glance at his lover confirmed Jonty's suspicions that Orlando was mulling over the very same thing.

"We were wondering..." it was the first time Cohen had spoken after his initial greeting and "thank you" for the refreshments, although he still couldn't quite look his hosts in the eye, "...why you seem to find yourselves so close to violent death so often?"

Orlando wouldn't be silenced on this occasion. "We didn't ask to be involved with that first case. I seem to remember that you requested our assistance and it was the same this time. We were asked because of our previous successes, as you might term them, to take an interest. The affair on Jersey rather gave people the impression that we could help out where matters weren't clear."

Orlando clearly enjoyed being able to say this. The case of Ainslie's father's death had been one in which he and Jonty were constantly one step ahead of the police, Wilson included.

The inspector tipped his head in acknowledgement. "That's a fair point."

"One might ask—" Orlando was in a particularly bullish mood now, "—why *you're* here and not the Metropolitan police."

"We've been asked to find some information for them. As you're not actually suspects, they felt it would be more apt if we dealt with things." Wilson glanced from one man to the other, a look in his eye that was now more beseeching than inquisitorial. "Dr. Stewart, Dr. Coppersmith, will you share with us what you know, so that we can instruct our colleagues?"

Orlando looked at his friend, who nodded agreement without a second thought. They told the police all they'd found out on their two journeys to London, omitting only the personal connection that the two victims had to their investigators. While mentioning Taylor's desire to confess some sin, they left the nature of the misdemeanour unqualified.

They emphasised that everything had been passed on to Collingwood, who'd promised to bring any matter of importance to the notice of the local police force. "And, I might add, the constabulary in Surrey would have saved themselves a lot of trouble if they'd been interested in what Mr. Cartwright had to say." There was a hint of relish in Orlando's voice. "Including what's quite possibly the arrest of the wrong man."

"I cannot comment officially on my opinion regarding the handling of this case. But strictly off the record I will tell you that I, we, aren't impressed." The tone in Wilson's voice left no one in any doubt that, if he'd been in charge of the officer who'd so carelessly disregarded such vital information, the man would have found himself blacking boots or sweeping chimneys. There was a renewed glint in his eye. "I wouldn't mind getting one up on that snooty lot down in Surrey. It's as well that you *were* called in or else no one would have sought to connect the two crimes, unless they somehow found out about that argument the two men had. If the crimes are linked, then the fact that Alistair Stafford couldn't possibly have committed the second murder might shed doubt on his being guilty of the first." All present nodded their agreement.

"Jardine and Taylor have a lot more in common than arguing in a club and being murdered within weeks of each other. Something that goes a long way back." Jonty's words cut the air like a knife. They'd reached a turning point in the case. He was nervous, nauseous, determined—having taken another step in what had been an unavoidable journey, inevitable once someone had killed Christopher Jardine. He respected and trusted both these officers, even if they'd appeared, at least fleetingly, to suspect him. "Do you remember that unfortunate lad at St. Bride's and why he did what he did?"

The inspector and sergeant nodded in unison. Who could forget the poor benighted young man who'd suffered terrors at school at the hands of one of his masters, and who'd taken terrible revenge years later, not on the perpetrator, but on men of a similar inclination?

"I had a comparable experience at school. I was used, abused, hurt, and there were two perpetrators. Taylor and Jardine." A silence lay over the room, broken only by the deafening ticking of that bloody clock. Jonty looked defiantly from one officer to the other. Orlando watched his lover, Cohen studied his shoes.

Wilson contemplated his steepled fingers then sighed. "Dr. Stewart, I appreciate the candour with which you've addressed us—it can't have been easy to make such an admission. I assume you understand this gives you a motive for wanting revenge on both these men?"

"I do realise. And I also know that I'm wholly innocent, as is my friend." Jonty's fists clenched and unclenched. "We have, as you pointed out, an immaculate alibi for yesterday and also one for the first of February, when we were at High Table in the presence of the vice chancellor."

"You're lucky that you move in such notable circles, although I seem to remember that you're the one who has no time for alibis." Wilson was well aware of the belligerence beneath Jonty's smooth exterior. "I'm grateful, nonetheless, that you can be vouched for. I was never convinced you were implicated in these deaths, although you do have an annoying habit of being in the vicinity of murders. Please, for all our sakes, let us know in future when you've been consulted."

"We will." Orlando was less cantankerous now that the police recognised his and Jonty's professional involvement. "I have something that might interest you, if you have a hankering for Taylor's fingerprints. We got them on Saturday and were going to bring them to you tomorrow. Even your Surrey colleagues might want to see if he'd been at the scene of Jardine's murder." Orlando, with great relish, explained how he'd obtained the little gems.

"Very ingenious, Dr. Coppersmith; I shall have to try that." Wilson took the case, he and Orlando drifting into a discussion on the arcane art of fingerprinting, then moving on to Bertillon and his measurement system.

Jonty may have found this a relief from the interrogation but it was equally tiring. He really needed his bed, his lover and some peace—his nerves were feeling shot to pieces again, to the point of wondering how much more of this wretched case he could take. *All the time one step forwards and two steps back.*

Orlando—dear, kind Orlando—noticed and immediately whisked the police away with many promises about telling all once Mr. Cartwright had provided the goods.

When he returned from the door, Jonty had already gone upstairs. He was to be located bundled up in his lover's bed, no glasses and no book, just waiting to talk.

"Orlando, I'm so glad we didn't tell Mama about this case." Jonty snuggled into his lover's arms, still uneasy, as he'd been since the police had knocked on the door.

Orlando swallowed hard, a wave of guilt starting to move up his spine. "Why's that, pup?"

"Because if she knew why we'd been to visit Taylor, the *whole truth* I mean, and the police knew that she knew, we'd never have been able to keep it secret from them. She'd be under suspicion, too." Jonty shivered, even though the evening wasn't yet that cold and the rain which murmured against the windows suggested it might stay mild.

Orlando held his lover tighter, wishing this wretched case had never come along to disrupt their blissful existence. "Jonty, don't worry. She has an alibi for Sunday morning, as we do."

"If anyone could arrange to appear to be in two places at once it would be my mother. And you know as well as I do that she'd be quite capable of smashing in my tormentor's head, then sailing off to confess it all and receive absolution." Jonty sighed, lay back, rubbed his head as if trying to make all the unpleasant thoughts disappear. "If I didn't feel entirely loved and cherished by her she'd scare the pants off me."

"Jonty..." Orlando swallowed hard. "She knows."

"Knows what?"

"That the case we're working on involves one of those boys from school."

Jonty shot bolt upright, shaking with emotion both in body and voice. "How? Did you tell her? Oh, how could you?"

Orlando addressed the bedspread, far too unsettled and guilty to face his lover. "She found you, Jonty, when there was the storm in London—she found you when you'd *gone elsewhere*. It frightened her silly. I had to explain, there were no means by which I could leave her in doubt. You do know that I wouldn't just betray your secrets?"

"I do. And I can well believe that she wangled as much of the detail out of you as she could. She's a sly old puss at times. I'm sorry for upbraiding you." The tension in Jonty's shoulders began to dissipate, only to return with a vengeance. "Oh Lord, does Papa know as well?"

"Not unless your mother has told him and I did ask her not to. If your blessed father had Jardine's name he'd have a starting point in looking for Taylor and Rhodes. Not that it would make any difference to the Honourable Timothy now. Lucky your papa was at church too."

"He has the best alibi of all. Someone could perhaps impersonate me or you but the royal family have known Father since he was a mere slip of a lad and couldn't be hoodwinked." Jonty sighed, burying his face in his lover's shoulder. "I just want this case to be finished as soon as possible. I was sure that Taylor had some involvement in Jardine's death, but now it looks as if there's at least one unknown party who might have killed either or both."

Orlando reached for the notebook he always kept by his bed. One by each bed, *just in case*. "Let's work this through then—we'll both feel the better for it. Matthew asked us to clear Alistair Stafford's name by solving

Jardine's murder. Now Taylor is dead and Stafford couldn't possibly have done that deed. While we have to consider the possibility that the two deaths are no more than a coincidence, we should pursue both cases in the belief that they're likely to be related."

Jonty nodded, a broad, unexpected grin lighting up his sapphire blue eyes. "I do like your best, stuffy 'let's study the case' tones. Find them ridiculously exciting, really, although I suppose that will have to wait. Let's keep our eyes firmly on what we know and not go off on the track of idle speculation, unless we have enough cause to go along a siding as 'twere. I mean I know you have your suspicions about Angela Stafford, but we've no reason to connect her to Timothy Taylor, so we must discount her at present." Jonty stabbed at his lover's chest. "And yes, I know that secretly you'd love it to be her. We must leave it to Collingwood's men to see whether that's a hare worth coursing."

Orlando sighed. For some reason he'd got it into his head that he rather wanted Angela to be guilty. It would take all the pressure off Jonty, for one thing, so when the case came to court there could be no mention of Jardine's argument with Taylor and the man who was the subject of it. "Fine. We know there's a connection between the men—not just the rather attractive one who's at my side looking outrageously seductive, but the fact that they were at school together and had obviously kept in touch. We know that milord was planning to leave the country and that Taylor was unhappy about it. Was someone else equally aggrieved with both of them?"

"Like another victim, do you mean? The timing of the deaths being a coincidence rather than linked to Jardine's proposed flight? It might work." Jonty ruffled his hair, lost in thought.

Orlando hastily studied his notes, or else nothing would get discussed. It was distracting enough having someone so attractive at your side while you were trying to think. When they were making themselves look young and helpless it made things almost impossible. Especially when you had the memory of a failed attempt at lovemaking to contend with. "Either a victim or another enemy they'd both made?"

Jonty tapped the notes his lover had written. "There is another way the deaths could connect. Jardine had a family, he didn't just emerge from the primeval swamp. I've met his mother once and while she doesn't strike me as likely to take up a poker to avenge her son's murderer, assuming Taylor was the murderer…"

"You're blethering again."

"Am not." Jonty slapped his lover's arm. "Listen. It's not inconceivable that one of milord's family felt the need to *do in* his killer."

"That's a point." Orlando noted it down. It had struck him from the start that it was a valid theory, but he was feeling incongruously frisky and wanted to niggle Stewart a bit. It often had desirable consequences, the sort of consequences he greatly desired at present. "Any other possible connections?"

Now Jonty found the bedspread to be of immense interest. "There is someone I could name who would have been very interested in what was said between those men at Platt's."

Orlando screwed up his nose, unable to see where the line of reasoning was going. "Who?"

"Oh, you are being so obtuse, do I have to spell it out? The master of St. Vincent house, Rhodes. We need to find him and know what he's been up to. While I don't look forward to it, it has to be done." Jonty picked at the coverlet, his wan face etched with discomfort.

"We'll set Collingwood onto getting an address. In the morning." Orlando laid down his book and pen, freeing hands to take his lover back into his arms. "Tonight we'll forget about it."

"You might be able to, but I can't. It's going to be with me all the time now, like a shadow at the back of my mind. It'll be there until the matter's all cleared up." Jonty's blue eyes looked dim, all the *joie de vivre* he normally showed hidden. Lost, like the evening sun had been as the rain clouds gathered. "Hold me tight and tell me things will get better one day."

While Orlando obliged to the best of his ability, he wasn't sure that either of them believed it.

Chapter Seven

"A mathematical whattery?"

"A mathematical conclave. It's been called at short notice to discuss a revolutionary theory before it gets published." Orlando waved his arms, recreating integral signs, or some such nonsense, in the air. It certainly enlivened the atmosphere of the breakfast table, even if it threatened to send the coffeepot flying.

Jonty laid his head to one side. His lover really wasn't a good liar and the truth would come out sooner or later, but if Orlando wanted to have a few days away then that suited him very well. He had his own fish to fry and an admirable co-fryer in the shape of his father. "When will you be back?"

"Oh, in a couple of days. Definitely by the twentieth. Plenty of time to get this case wrapped up." Orlando hid his nose in his coffee cup, trying to cover up his guilty expression. "And I notice you've got the calendar down to scrutinise. What are you up to? Checking when my suit's ready so that you can put me on a plinth and have the whole thing unveiled in the Old Court?"

"Nearly." Jonty smiled, his humour a bit better now than the night before and his wits in no way dimmed. He knew when attention was being deflected. "We can pick your wonderful new outfit up on the twenty-seventh, en route to Mama's. That's the Wednesday in Holy Week, isn't it?"

"Put your spectacles on if you can't see the writing." Orlando dodged out of the way of the slap which always followed a *glasses* remark.

"I shall stick my spectacles up your backside if you continue to make fun of them. You'll need them too one day and then the boot will be well and truly on the other foot. I knew all along about the dates, I was making polite conversation—unlike some people who are satisfied with a grunt and a harrumph." Jonty tapped the calendar, as if to prove he could see it perfectly well. He wasn't going to admit to the fact that it was slightly blurry round the edges. "What I mean is that we'll only have two and a bit weeks to get ourselves into a reasonable state. There's precious little time between Easter and the start of next term. Less than we'd counted on."

"Then we need to have this affair pretty well cracked before we go down to Sussex." Orlando marked the days off with his finger. "Seems awful to say it, but for once I won't be looking forward to seeing your dear mama. Not if it means that we get behind on this case and can't help Matthew's friend."

The use of Ainslie's Christian name was a novelty—Jonty studied his lover. "Are we softening a bit, Mr. Coppersmith? You were noticeably friendlier when we met for lunch that Sunday."

"Matthew is a fine man, and now I'm certain that he won't try any funny business with either of us I'm quite happy to oblige him. And there's the thrill of the chase, of course." Orlando grinned.

Jonty did the same, recognising how much his lover appreciated the challenge of solving a problem where the outcome really mattered. The higher mathematics was all well and good, but here a man's life was at stake and that was much more important.

Later, when he thought back on things, Jonty was sure this was the point at which their luck in the case changed. Maybe the angels were looking down and being kind. Maybe the imminent departure of the dunderheads to their homes, where they could be feted and spoiled by their mothers and not have to think too hard, allowed the wheels of the universe to move more rapidly. Whatever the cause, the inhabitants of Forsythia Cottage went from having frustratingly little information to receiving a glut of it.

The first item came two days after the police had visited, and was in the form of a letter, written in a bold hand—the postmark suggested Mr. Cartwright. Jonty opened it over breakfast, immediately beginning to read aloud. *"Dear Dr. Coppersmith and Dr. Stewart—"*

"He obviously recognises whom he should address as the superior. Ow!"

"I am delighted to try to assist you in this case. My wife tells me that you were most gracious to her when you visited Dorking and that she would be proud for us to be of service to what, you assure her, is an innocent man. She was charmed by us, Orlando. It was probably the way I complimented those sponge cakes. *I only wish that our local peelers, if you will excuse so gross a term, were more polite or interested in what a common man has to say. I'm confident that you'll find it of interest."*

"Of course we will—get on with it, Jonty."

"I'm glad to have had a while to think things through. When I first considered that night, I believed that I saw one man visiting; now I remember that there were two."

"Well there's something to get our teeth into at last."

"Let me be as plain as I can. At about eleven o'clock I'd got up to let our old spaniel out for a few minutes to do what was necessary, if you'll excuse the expression. There was a young man coming down the drive, walking very briskly. He passed me by without a word and set off towards the town. I thought little of it at the time, being used to all sorts of comings and goings at the House and having been sure I heard this man arrive earlier, when I was finishing my pipe. That gravel path is very useful for keeping you abreast of who's around."

"Can't you read a bit faster? Shall I fetch your strongest spectacles?"

"I'll go slower now. *I. Went. Back. To. Bed.* Oof! That was unfair. In boxing you'd forfeit the round for a low blow. *And I now recall that I'd heard someone else coming up the drive about an hour before this man I saw; it was when I was reading the newspaper, although I only was aware of one of them leaving. I'd forgotten all about the first man, me being such a chump, if you'll excuse my coarseness. It sounded like he had a limp. There was something halt about the way he crunched over the gravel, anyway."*

"This is more like it, Jonty. Something positive to go on."

"I didn't hear him return, but it might have happened when I was asleep of course. I have no idea whether this is related to the murder. You're more learned than I am and I'm sure you can work it out. And that's all there is. Apart from some good wishes, an offer of further help and the usual pleasantries." Jonty laid the letter down on the table, disappointed.

"It's good stuff as far as it goes." Orlando picked up the correspondence to peruse it. "There seems nothing hole-and-corner about the people who are coming and going, walking bold as brass past that lodge rather than inching through the shrubbery. Which possibly fits in with the victim knowing, or at least being at ease with, his murderer. You don't let your enemy round the back of you with a poker."

"You might let Angela Stafford get close, though." Jonty hated to say it, but there was something to be said for Orlando's pet theory.

"No, I've been thinking about that some more. Jardine would have likely as not mistrusted her. He'd have suspected she was out for revenge. Unless she tried to, um—" Orlando fiddled with the letter, "— butter him up."

"Is 'butter him up' a euphemism for 'seduce'? Still, it's a good point. Unless he was overpowered in some other way first, and then the poker applied."

Orlando shrugged, eloquently. They didn't know enough and there was no point speculating. "I'm sure this must work in Stafford's favour. I don't think that he has a limp—Matthew will be able to tell us."

"Irrespective of whether Stafford possesses a gammy leg, I can think of someone who has, or did have."

"Not that chap your mother invited to dinner? I won't believe in such a coincidence."

"No, chump. Anyway, I shan't play the three guesses game, as my heart's not in it. If you want someone a bit halt in one leg, look no further than my old housemaster, Rhodes. Seeing Rex limping that evening triggered my memory and got me all upset. On top of the thunder and all…" Jonty's voice trailed away.

Orlando turned the subject to Mr. Cartwright's unique writing style.

The second piece of enlightenment came in the form of a telephone call from Collingwood, returning one he'd had from Coppersmith in the wake of Cartwright's letter. The harsh ringing of the bell found the fellows busily trying to tie up all the loose ends of the Lent term and preparing for the Easter, especially Orlando, who had a potential Senior Wrangler among his usual dimwits.

According to the solicitor, Alistair Stafford was still assuring all and sundry that he'd not gone to Dorking the night of the murder. He'd pointed out that if he'd taken his horse, as he would have been obliged to do in order to cover the distance, he'd not have needed to walk up the drive. And, of course, he'd been incapable of killing Taylor—of whom he vowed he had no knowledge—being incarcerated at the time.

"Collingwood also said that Angela Stafford has no alibi for the second murder, although no motive either." There was a note of glee in Orlando's voice, as he related the conversation to his lover. "Her alibi for the first one is apparently unshakable, so I suppose she has to be eliminated from all sensible enquiry."

"Unless we find ourselves in the midst of some farfetched shilling shocker where the most unlikely chain of events occur." Jonty raised his hand to end the debate. "And please don't remind me that I'm the one who doesn't trust alibis. I wish I'd never confessed to it. Is there any more about Taylor?"

"Collingwood's contacts say the man went out the night before he was killed, although no one seems to know where."

"I only hope he was meeting someone with a ruddy limp."

Jonty rang his father during the evening, when Orlando was out at his bridge club. He'd been mulling things over all day and had come to a momentous decision—although he didn't want his lover involved, just yet.

Once the case was fully explained, Richard Stewart was quite clear about what was required, not least in terms of the delicacy which surrounded things. Jonty swore his father not to reveal to anyone else the names he'd been given, although now, with two of the men dead, he supposed there was little point in keeping the identities of his abusers hidden.

After making his papa swear he wouldn't go in pursuit of Rhodes, Jonty came to the crux of his call. "Do you think there might be any evidence that other boys suffered at the hands of this evil triumvirate? It would probably be before my time, or maybe concurrent with it. Aren't you all pally with the present Headmaster?"

"He's a good man. Do you want me to question him?" The excitement in Mr. Stewart's voice was evident, even down the crackling phone line.

"If you would. You could find out whether he had any lingering suspicions about what went on under his predecessor. Wasn't he a master when I was there? I vaguely remember the name."

"Dr. Barrington? He was. He's probably got an inkling or two to be shared. As long, no doubt, as no cloud gets spread over the present day school." Old bloodhound Stewart was delighted to be given such an important assignment. "Give me a day or two and I'll report back."

*

The call came, full of juicy information, to the cottage the day before Orlando's departure for his supposed conclave. "Jonty?" Mr. Stewart's voice boomed down the line.

"No need to shout, Papa, it's a telephone, not a megaphone."

"Safe to talk?"

"Yes. *He's* had to go to Bride's to see Dr. Peters about one of the students. What's the news?"

"The news is that you were quite right. Dr. Barrington says there were several boys he'd been concerned about, and one of them was indeed the lad who was killed in that so-called accident. Barrington was only a young master at the time, yet he'd been deeply troubled. The other teachers and the Headmaster had fobbed him off with the usual nonsense. *Nothing suspicious in it at all. Such a terrible tragedy, Nicholls falling onto such a sharp blade*, but he'd not been convinced. He'd guessed the lad in question might have been intensely unhappy and something had driven him to take his own life."

"Could he put a name to it?" Jonty slid into the small chair they kept in the hall. He felt cold, colder than he'd have been outside in the brisk East Anglian wind.

"Not at the time. Later he understood what could go on at boarding schools and then the penny dropped. However, as you know, Jardine and Taylor weren't at the school at the time of Nicholls' alleged suicide, so they couldn't have been to blame. That beast Rhodes was there, though, and the boy was in his house. He was said to be friendly with the lad's family."

"Did you…" The knot in Jonty's throat made every word agony.

"No. I just said I was concerned with events which might have sullied what, after all, was *my* old school too. If Barrington knew about what happened to you he didn't show any sign of it. He did talk about a second boy, though, another one in Rhodes's house. He'd been withdrawn by his mother with much shouting in the Head's study and letters to the governing body, apparently. I think you must have been at the school then, although the boy's name doesn't ring a bell."

"Did Barrington do anything on that occasion?" Jonty wanted to rail against anyone who stood by and let the innocent suffer. All hell's demons were not enough for them.

"He told me he wanted to, and I believe him. But he came down with bloody—don't you dare tell your mother I swore—appendicitis, had an operation, ended up with complications and was in convalescence for over a year. By the time he returned, everything had been smoothed over and none of it had been made public. After you left, he was appointed Headmaster by a radicalised governing body who wanted a younger man at the helm. One who would sweep the rats from the deepest decks of this once noble ship. It was then he found out that a payment had been made to this second lad's family, a bribe to ensure they kept silent, no doubt, though the source of the money hadn't been school coffers."

"Whew." Jonty whistled down the phone, almost deafening his father in the process.

"Manners, Jonty! What would your mama say? Anyway Barrington swept away the rats, including Rhodes. More importantly for your investigation, he gave me that other lad's name. Simon Kermode."

"Papa, you're a marvel."

He was better than that. Mr. Stewart had even, and how he'd managed it his son never fathomed, obtained an address for Kermode in Norwich, which was a nice easy run from Cambridge. Jonty felt obliged to ask his father to accompany him but he'd demurred, stating that the presence of two men at any interview wouldn't be conducive to absolute candour.

The angels, or whoever was smiling on him at present, then dispensed another piece of good fortune, this time in the form of Mrs. Ward. Although luck wouldn't really have been an appropriate description, more like perspicacity. The lady knew a lot about Norwich, having lived there twice. She had, like so many kind and garrulous women, soon acquired an intimate knowledge of the city, its characters and their goings-on. Whoever envisaged espionage agents as being ideally cerebral, dashing young men or glamorous, mysterious ladies had underestimated the potential of middle-aged women as finders and interpreters of information.

"Of course I know the Kermodes, Dr. Stewart. I'd say the son's perhaps a little foppish and spoiled, no doubt the effect of an overbearing mother."

Jonty, who was the son of an equally domineering woman, had to bite into a cake at this point to hide his grin.

"Simon inherited his father's estate and his debts. Mother and son ended up in a villa, I suppose you'd call it genteel, with an antique bookshop near the cathedral. We all thought he'd fail, but that business thrived. The last thing I heard, they were moving into a bigger house and talking of establishing a shop in London, of all places." Mrs. Ward's frown eloquently expressed her opinion of both London and the Kermodes.

All this suited Jonty's plans to perfection. It would be natural for the Kildare Fellow in Tudor Literature to want to look for rare texts—Richard Barnfield might be one to work into the mix—and from there they could move onto other subjects. Especially if they discovered, *quite by chance*, that they went to the same school and if he offered to stand lunch. Alcohol might well loosen a tongue.

The trip to Norwich wasn't a long one. Jonty enjoyed looking out over the flat landscape, staring and thinking of very little, although he wondered what "old grumpy breeches" was up to. It was unlike Orlando to be quite so secretive. There was an uneasy feeling at the back of Jonty's brain that he knew exactly what his lover was about—or *who* he was about, to be more precise, but he tried hard to ignore it. He had his own work to do.

Once off the train and out of the station, he decided to skirt the city, electing to take a walk along the river—pretty, but not a patch on the Cam—coming to the cathedral widdershins and finding the bookshop with no difficulty. Between them, his father and housekeeper could have guided a man to all the sources of the Nile. The shop was small, its stock clearly beginning to outgrow it, although it was well lit through scrupulously clean leaded windows.

If Timothy Taylor looked to have aged thirty years in fifteen, then Kermode appeared to have stayed much the same as he'd have been at school. Given that the man was older than Jonty, he looked ridiculously young and there was hardly a piece of fluff on his face. While the Kildare Fellow blethered on about books, he also spent a minute wondering if Kermode actually needed to shave yet.

They did have a Barnfield in stock, although it was a heavily bowdlerised version, and when Jonty turned it down Kermode was impressed, at least professionally, with his acumen.

The small talk flowed, each sentence edging Jonty nearer his goal. This he reached when Kermode told his assistant that this customer was an old school chum who had to be entertained for an hour or so. As they walked through the busy streets, it struck Jonty that Kermode had exactly the same colouring and build as he had—they must have looked similar when at school. The uneasy thought flitted through his brain that Christopher Jardine might have had a taste for the type.

The Stewart smile and the Stewart money ensured them a table at the best restaurant they could find, at a hotel which had once been a coaching inn and still had the galleries to prove it. In a room which had probably changed little in a hundred years, they were entertained royally with a selection of excellent food and wines. The Chablis proved so effective in oiling Kermode's tongue that once the reluctant bolt had been loosened the flow couldn't be stemmed.

They spoke of the recent murders, quite naturally, then turned to their own memories of school. It only needed the most oblique of references from Jonty to the unpleasantness of their former housemaster to produce a stream of vitriol.

"Sebastian Rhodes was an absolute bastard, did you know that?" Kermode lowered his voice in deference to their public location. "He made my short sojourn at school an absolute nightmare. Not him personally of

Lessons in Power

course, he wouldn't have sullied his hands or any other part of his anatomy with actual contact, but..."

Stewart froze. A cold sensation was creeping up his spine, making him feel by turns sick and excited. He'd anticipated having to worm and wheedle to get Kermode to talk, yet they were getting close to the crux of the matter in hand with hardly any effort expended. He felt suddenly wary, as if *he* were the one falling into the trap. "I did know, Simon. I had personal experience of it, if you get my drift."

"You too? I should have guessed that someone else would cop it once I'd gone. He couldn't go without his thrills for too long."

The almost exact repetition of his own phrase made Jonty even colder and more ill at ease. He'd often said the same thing to Orlando, and now it was becoming a self-fulfilling prophesy. "You're right. It got to the point that I'd have given anything for a convenient gun, although whether it was to shoot them or myself I don't recall."

Jonty did remember of course. There would have been three bullets needed, not one, but he was becoming good at acting, if required.

"I used to devise tortures for them. Not just at the time—on many an occasion since. Ways to make them suffer as I did." Kermode stopped, focussing hazy eyes on Jonty for the first time since they'd started on this subject. "As we did." He seemed as if he was thinking hard, a process the alcohol was making difficult.

"I can't help admitting to similar fantasies." Jonty grinned, although he was uneasy at the look in Kermode's eye.

"When Jardine was killed, were you down in Dorking?"

The abruptness of the question stunned Jonty. The tables were being turned on him again and it wasn't comfortable. "No, I was not. I happened to be at High Table if you must know, not many miles from here. Why do you ask?"

"Just wondered. I was there, you know." Kermode offered this astonishing fact as simply as if he'd mentioned a visit to the grocer. "I wondered whether it was you there as well. Whether you'd come here to tell me that you'd..."

That brought Jonty up short again. This must be why he felt so uncomfortable—Kermode suspected *him*, rather than vice versa—and he wasn't sure how to handle the revelation. He changed tack. "What did you talk to Jardine about?" He had no great hopes for an accurate answer.

Kermode was showing signs of sobering up, but not enough to guarantee the veracity of what he had to say.

"About *it*, what had happened back in school." A strange look came over Kermode's face as if even *he* doubted the truth of what he was saying. "It seems that Jardine was having a crisis of conscience. He told me he'd had a 'road to Damascus' experience and realised he had to come clean about the whole sorry business. He wanted to make some sort of public apology to the people he'd wronged—there'd been quite a few down the years, not just at school—and then quietly leave the country."

"Did you believe any of this?"

"Surprisingly enough, I did. I knew the man could lie, we both know that, but this time he seemed in deadly earnest. He said he'd been in touch with Taylor and tried to persuade him to do the same. He'd been refused, of course, and they'd ended up in a blazing row at his lordship's club."

The whole case had turned upside down. Jonty and Orlando had cheerfully assumed that what Taylor had said was the truth, that *he* was the one who wanted to confess, who felt so weighed down by the burden of his sins that he wanted to be shot of them. They'd accepted as fact that Jardine had tried to talk him out of it and had planned to leave the country when Taylor made his confession.

Now they had to consider the exact reverse. If Taylor had been the one who'd argued for their misdemeanours not to come to light, it gave him an ample motive for the killing. Had he been down to Dorking, as they'd always suspected, killed Jardine and so given himself some breathing space? Nothing in the case so far argued against it. Even the lameness of the man Mr. Cartwright heard on the gravel could be accounted for by Taylor's poor physical condition.

What about his lordship's sea change concerning his disreputable youth? Had the man really had some sort of conversion experience? Jonty found it unlikely, given his experience of Jardine, and especially in light of his recent treatment of Angela Stafford. However, it would certainly be just like the swine to make a clean breast of things and then immediately bugger off to the continent before the manure hit the fan.

Jonty couldn't deny even the most miserable of sinners the right to repentance. He had known it happen—Richard Marsters had told him of many an occasion when a similar thing had occurred—and sometimes the men involved made Christopher Jardine look like an angel.

"Dr. Stewart, what do you think?" Kermode had been blithely rambling on while Jonty's mind whirred into the past and the future and all sorts of places between.

"I'm so very sorry, I was woolgathering. Please be so kind as to say it again and forgive my inattention."

Kermode smiled. He assumed that Jonty's mind had been back in the cold cruel dormitories at school and was willing to forgive him any lack of consideration. "Do you think that Taylor might have killed Jardine? To stop him telling all and thereby to protect himself."

"It's at least possible." Jonty eyed the other man. "Did you by any chance go and see Taylor? To get his point of view?"

Suddenly, unexpectedly, the shutters came down. "I had nothing to say to Timothy Taylor." Kermode pressed his lips together, his face growing as hard as the horse brasses which graced the restaurant.

It was immediately apparent to Jonty that he'd get no more from him, no matter how hard he tried. It was now a matter of finishing their coffee, shaking hands and parting.

As the train wended its way back to Cambridge, Jonty began to speculate again. Even if they had a potential solution to who had killed Jardine, the murder of Taylor himself remained a mystery. If he had killed his lordship, then revenge by a member of Jardine's family became a possibility, although that all felt too disconnected. The solution must be simpler.

A vague recollection of what Mrs. Ward had said about Kermode's mother flitted through Jonty's mind, making him wonder whether she might have seen fit to take a poker to the head of the man who'd hurt her beloved boy. She certainly seemed likely to have had the gumption, and it would explain the man's reluctance to discuss the second victim. Whatever the truth, they still hadn't got to the bottom of this wretched case.

Chapter Eight

There had actually been two letters from Collingwood delivered to Forsythia Cottage, one addressed to Dr. Coppersmith alone, which he'd squirreled away. According to the solicitor's sources, Rhodes was alive, well and living in Epsom, not far from the racecourse. He was within easy distance of the railway, in the house of a devoted maiden aunt who kept a carriage and probably let her nephew have free rein of it.

Orlando had immediately made what would, no doubt, turn out to be either an inspired or disastrous decision. He wouldn't tell his lover.

Jonty was fragile at present, despite all his bravado and insistence that he had to confront his own demons. Orlando was determined that he alone should make the running here—only when he'd seen Rhodes and drawn the man's fangs would he allow Jonty to get anywhere near him.

If there was anything left of him to get near. Orlando hated his lover's old schoolmaster even more than he hated the boys who'd carried out the assaults. They might just, hypothetically, with a fair wind, have left the boy alone had Rhodes not egged them on. And Rhodes had been *in loco parentis*, a position that shouldn't have been abused, especially not on *his* Jonty.

So he'd invented the nonexistent mathematical seminar and felt satisfied he'd pulled the wool over his friend's eyes on that one. The plan, as he assembled it, was to spend a day or two snooping around Epsom, talking to Rhodes and his neighbours, then beating the man's head to a pulp. Or that would be the ideal plan—murder really shouldn't feature, not least because Jonty would spifflicate him. He'd have to restrain himself, reluctantly, when the time came.

When the time *did* come it caught Orlando by the lee. Meeting Taylor had left him surprised, preconceptions all askew, but meeting the ringleader of the repellent gang of three shook his ideas to pieces. The attractive house up on Epsom Downs, where old Miss Rhodes lived with her favourite nephew, impressed him—a neat, well-kept property with pleasant views and even more pleasant servants. Orlando had expected Rhodes to be a snivelling wretch, like the man he'd met in London, but

Jonty's old housemaster was far from that. He was charming, handsome still in middle age, attentive to his aunt and to their unexpected guest.

Orlando simply announced to the butler that he was here on behalf of Mr. Collingwood and left the rest to speculation. Rhodes welcomed him in, offering tea and chatting as if they were old friends, then letting the old lady act as hostess, something which she obviously relished.

The conversation flowed with relative ease, the only uncomfortable moment being when the chatelaine started, out of the blue, to relate an encounter she'd had with a ghost, a tale which appeared to unnerve Rhodes, possibly because it demonstrated his elderly relative's slightly tenuous grasp of reality.

He invited his guest into his study, "So that we may discuss business, Aunt," ushered the man into a comfortable chair then sat at his desk, smiling with great charm. If Orlando hadn't known the whole sordid truth, this façade would have taken him in—no wonder Rhodes had got away with things so easily.

"I'm here to see if you can be of help regarding the tragic murders of two of your old pupils," Orlando began, more civilly than he felt.

"Lord Christopher Jardine and the Honourable Timothy Taylor? If there is anything I can do to help bring their murderers—or perhaps murderer, single, I might infer from your tone—to justice, I would be honoured so to do."

"Then you might begin by answering me a question. Where were you on the morning of Sunday the tenth of March?"

"I was here." Rhodes's sweeping gesture seemed to take in the whole estate. "My aunt will verify that. As she wasn't well enough to go to church, I stayed with her. I won't ask you why you need to know the answer. I have read about the detective exploits of Dr. Coppersmith and Dr. Stewart."

Orlando bridled at the blatant mention of Jonty's name, but still made a mental note to check all the train timetables, to see how quickly a trip to London and back could have been made on the Sunday morning Taylor was killed. He didn't think there was any point in talking to Auntie. She appeared to be having a few problems remembering what had happened ten minutes since, let alone a week or more.

"And had you seen Mr. Taylor at all, recently?" Orlando produced an impressive-looking notepad and pen, unscrewing the lid of the latter in a theatrical manner as he prepared to make observations. It diverted his immediate thoughts away from those concerning Rhodes's nose and contact with *his* fist.

"I have, on the Saturday evening, the day before his murder. He'd rung me in the afternoon as he had things he wished to discuss. Now don't look so surprised, Dr. Coppersmith—there are certain of my ex- pupils with whom I have kept in fairly constant contact, offering an avuncular ear when required. Taylor was one." Rhodes smiled, looking just like a kindly uncle.

"How often did you speak with him?" Orlando forced the words out.

"Not often. We usually corresponded, both of us being fonder of the pen than this contraption." Rhodes indicated the phone. "And we don't have the opportunity to meet face-to-face as often as we might wish."

Orlando felt sick. This man was so smooth, so plausible, he couldn't work out whether any of what Rhodes said was true or just a fabrication. Or some clever mixture of the two. He fiddled with his pen again, took in some of the surroundings. Nothing seemed of particular significance, except for a picture on the desk of a young blond-haired man, not unhandsome, who might just have been a distant Stewart cousin. Orlando focussed on the matter in hand. "And what did he want to talk about?"

"He was having a crisis of conscience about something which had happened in his youth. I hope you won't ask me to divulge the nature of his problem, as it was told to me entirely in confidence." Rhodes smiled again, exuding the air of some wise Old Testament judge, at which point Orlando decided that he really did want to murder him. He could guess what the conversation with Taylor had been about and that his and Jonty's visit had prompted the call. Assuming Rhodes was telling the truth.

"You would tell the police, of course, should they feel it necessary to come and speak to you, as I shall suggest they do."

"I would tell the police everything they wanted to know. Like you, Dr. Coppersmith, I know what my duty is."

Orlando dragged his thoughts away from blunt instruments and the skulls of smarmy men. "Was his lordship one of the men with whom you kept in touch?"

"Not as much as I did with Taylor, but we did correspond occasionally." For once Rhodes looked a touch uneasy. "Would you like some more tea, or a glass of something? The sun is well over the yardarm." The man smiled, although Orlando knew that he'd sought to change the subject.

"No, thank you. When did you last see Lord Christopher?"

Lessons in Power

"The night he died, believe it or not. I must have been in the house when he was murdered." Rhodes had secured the chink in his armour and he'd adopted his bland, believable face again.

Orlando felt sick once more. He was either getting to the crux of the case or some strange web was being spun around him, of which he had no understanding. "Are you saying...?"

"Dr. Coppersmith, I'm sure you possess a facility for logic and reasoning. All I'm stating is that I was there, not that I committed the deed." Rhodes suddenly smiled, his persuasive air returning. "I'm being unfair, let me explain. I had arrived at the house earlier. His lordship wanted to discuss a matter related to the one Taylor later wanted to talk to me about. I understand they'd already had words over it. I assume you know that?"

Against his will, Orlando found himself nodding and being compliant— he recognised he was losing control of this interview and wasn't sure how to regain what Jonty, when he'd been reading Marryat, called 'the weather gage'. "Then why did the servants not remember you being there?"

"You are, I'm sure, a man of the world, Dr. Coppersmith. Much more than I am, with my sheltered background and quiet existence."

I'll kill him now and make it look like his aunt was responsible.

"You will therefore understand how Lord Christopher valued his privacy. His general rule, or so he told me, was to let all his guests in and out himself after dark. Not a normal practice for a gentleman but that was his whim. So I was not seen by the domestic servants, nor was the other visitor, who came after me."

"And did *you* see this other caller?" Orlando had decided that a knife would be too messy, bare hands too time consuming and making the man choke on his own teeth satisfying but not easy to pin on Auntie.

"Alas, no, or I could have provided the police with a description. His lordship made me retire to the library while he entertained this other individual. Now here's a conundrum for you. When I entered the house Jardine was alive and when I left it he was dead, yet I wasn't aware that this person or persons unknown had committed the deed."

Orlando fixed his enemy with a steely glare. "I don't wish to deal with conundrums, Mr. Rhodes. Please make yourself plain."

"I have teased you, sir, quite wrongly in so serious a case. I was talking to Christopher..."

Orlando noticed the slip into familiarity that suggested, along with the other signs, that Rhodes hadn't been entirely candid about the extent to which he knew Jardine.

"…when the door was knocked, and knocked very forcefully, I may add. His lordship at this point asked me to step into the library for a while, this room being on the other side of the hall from his drawing room. I waited there for the best part of an hour. There was plenty to read and keep myself occupied with. I believed I then heard the front door open and close, so prepared myself to be readmitted to my former pupil's presence. It did not happen. Eventually I simply let myself out."

"You didn't go and say goodbye to your host?"

"Dr. Coppersmith, as we said before, my host—as you call him—was a man of the world. He often had visitors in the evening who didn't take their leave until the morning. Not all of them were close friends nor did they use the guest apartments." As Rhodes spoke there was the merest hint of some emotion lurking beneath the smooth veneer. "You can imagine I would have assumed this is what had happened, so I felt discretion was called for. In any case we had said all we needed to."

"I thought you said you didn't know Jardine well? How can you be aware of so much intimate detail about his life?"

"I do not believe I said that at all, Dr. Coppersmith. You can verify it in your notes."

Orlando coloured, bridled—Rhodes had caught him out there. The great, gaping void at his side, the lack of his lover to help and support him, ached. It was a terrible shock to realise he could no longer function alone as efficiently as he'd done for so long before Jonty had burst into his life. He tapped his notes, ploughed on. "Then how did you know he was dead when you left? That's the crux of the conundrum you stated, is it not?"

Rhodes seemed unperturbed at being questioned so intensely. "As I returned to the station I was passed by a policeman cycling up to the house. I now assume he'd been summoned when the butler found the body. Certainly the details in the newspaper support this assumption."

"And why didn't you tell the police about this second visitor?"

"I am ashamed to admit that I was scared. I feared they would hear me confess that I was in the house and presuppose—as you have not, I take it, being a man who would rely on proof—I was the culprit. Besides, what could I say? I had only heard the door. I had no evidence from my own two eyes of whether it was even a male or female visitor. It would make my own story appear even more counterfeit."

Orlando contemplated long and hard, until he was sure he detected another sign of Rhodes's unease, although that might simply have been a matter of genuine social discomfort at the long delay in the conversation. His mind was whirling. He knew the truth about what this man had done to Jonty and how he had covered his tracks efficiently. Rhodes must be adept at spinning a yarn, embroidering a tale, making himself appear as credible as possible. Was he employing such techniques now? Orlando simply couldn't tell, and he regretted again that Jonty wasn't by his side. *He* might well have seen through the outer façade of reason and into the cold heart of the monster. "Is everything you have told me the truth?" It was a feeble assay and Orlando knew it.

"It is, Dr. Coppersmith. Not a word of a lie."

*

"So you went to see Rhodes. Without me. I knew it," Jonty snapped, awash with anger. "All that nonsense about a mathematical meeting—I guessed where you'd gone, I just didn't admit it to myself."

"I didn't want you hurt any more. Not after seeing what you were like when Wilson and Cohen were here. Anyway, you went to see Kermode without telling me." Orlando knew he'd handled this all wrong. Even when he'd shared his knowledge about Rhodes being in Jardine's house it had only provoked more annoyance. Though whether that had been partly because it scuppered Jonty's lovely theory about Taylor, he couldn't be sure. Attack now seemed his only way of defence.

"It's not the same case at all. Kermode wasn't one of my *bêtes noires*. He was just a source of information."

"But you kept it all a secret. Why?"

"Don't try to change the subject and pin things on me, Orlando bloody Coppersmith. I'm not some poor maiden in a children's adventure who needs to be cosseted and sheltered. I can fight my own battles." Jonty certainly looked at that moment as if he'd never known fear or doubt. It would have been awe- inspiring had Orlando not known the truth.

"I only thought…"

"You think too much. Leave off." Jonty flapped away the hand that reached to touch him, then stormed from the room.

Orlando began to follow but thought better of it. One had to let Jonty have at least three-and-a-half minutes to calm down before it was worth broaching anything. Then one could go, spy on him and decide the next piece of strategy.

Orlando watched his lover stomping around the garden, kicking at stones and muttering to himself. He could think of no words to broach the situation or bring about a rapprochement. He'd made an error of judgement with Rhodes and now he was paying for it. Whatever he tried, he'd have to be canny about it.

As Jonty scuffed though the wet grass and launched a snail shell through the air with the toe of his boot, he suddenly felt an express train hit him between the shoulders. Or more precisely it hit him around the waist, taking him down in one of the most effective rugby tackles he'd ever undergone.

"Orlando, what the hell..." His words were stifled as he was kissed roughly and had his arms pinned down on the lawn.

"I won't let you up until I'm forgiven." Orlando kissed him again, and again, until Jonty started to giggle.

"You are so unfair. You know that you can't come and reason things out with me so you resort to dirty tactics. I always end up laughing and then I can't be angry with you."

"Say I'm forgiven." Orlando looked like a spaniel that had been chastised over a stolen piece of meat. "Kiss me again."

"Not till you say I'm forgiven." The spaniel's ears drooped.

"That's changing the tactics halfway through. Fine, I forgive you, Orlando, only do let me up, my pants are soaked through and Mrs. Ward will go mad when she sees the mud."

Orlando kissed Jonty as promised, and very nice it was, then brushed him down as best he could. "We should ring Wilson. He needs to come up and hear what we've found out."

"You do that. I'll organise a little something to give us strength for the ordeal."

Jonty found their housekeeper mending trouser cuffs. He enquired whether a pot of tea could be available when the constabulary arrived and if there might also be a cake blockaded in the pantry which could be let out.

Both enquiries being successful he was about to depart when a firm female voice said, "Dr. Stewart, I think you and Dr. Coppersmith had both better change your suits. You look like you've been searching for the sources of the Amazon. On foot."

*

"How on earth do you do it?" Wilson laid his hat on the sideboard and scratched his balding head. He thought he'd gone beyond amazement at these two, but they'd excelled themselves this time. "My colleagues have been trying all this time to put a name to one or other of those mysterious visitors. Then you find the pair of them simultaneously and without the slightest effort."

"That's not quite right. I'll admit we knew about Rhodes before, although we didn't have anything more than suspicion and hunches, certainly not enough to justify passing his name on to you. But finding Kermode involved a lot of legwork on Papa's behalf." Jonty wore a belligerent grin. He was enjoying getting one over on the police again, especially after their last meeting.

"Oh, so there are three of you involved now, are there? Holmes, Watson and Lestrade?"

"Cuff, Cuff and Cuff more like, although without the roses." Orlando was also enjoying the discomfort on his guests' faces. "Perhaps we can now restrict our investigations to two men."

"Unless there's a third unknown person who sneaked in through that shrubbery when the others were engaged, doing the deed in between Kermode leaving and Rhodes's departure. Your Mr. Taylor perhaps." Wilson grinned.

Jonty groaned. "I can't take it. It's more like some Drury Lane farce than real life, people coming and going everywhere. My mind can only cope with two entities and if you want to introduce a third I'll ignore it. Look, I had a perfectly clear theory. Kermode had gone to Dorking, where he confronted Jardine. Taylor was there already, got into another row about this imminent confession and did his lordship in. Kermode went home, confessed all to his mother, who then located Taylor and beat him up for not having repented. Mrs. Ward confirms that she's just the sort of woman to do it, which is as good as a judge's ruling."

"I'm afraid that all goes out of the window now we know it was Rhodes down in Dorking." Orlando spoke as if he were talking to a four-year-old, which made Jonty thump his arm.

"I know that, you clot, and I'm trying to work out a whole new theorem, sans Taylor. That's why I don't want him put back into the equation." He looked pleadingly at Wilson. "This is becoming far too complicated, isn't it? In our admittedly limited experience, murder tends to be relatively simple."

"And in mine," the inspector concurred. "So we have two men with Jardine, each of whom might have had cause to kill him, either in vengeance or to stop him making their secret public knowledge."

"But what about Taylor? We're still no nearer solving his murder, unless it really was Mrs. Kermode in avenging angel mode." Why was it that every step they took forward in this case was followed by another three back?

"What about Rhodes?" Sergeant Cohen suddenly spoke up, his large, bovine face becoming animated. "He might have worried that Taylor would be going to confess all, as well. Especially if he knew that you two had been to visit." The idea struck the company like a blow. No one had so far suggested that Jonty's call on Taylor might have acted as a catalyst in the man's demise.

"You're right," Jonty ventured at last. "We'd begun to stir up a hornet's nest, asking questions left right and centre. I wonder if it was old Rhodes who visited Waite's, as well, pretending to be a newspaper reporter. Now there's food for thought."

"I've some more things for you to chew over—you're not the only ones who can make progress, you know." Wilson smiled, enjoying the badinage and byplay with these two clever young men. It would make any policeman's job much more satisfying. "We've found out that two men were seen going into Taylor's house the morning he died. Not you two, I hasten to add." There was a puckish tone to his voice. "The first was a youngish chap. We'll have to see if you recognise the description as matching Kermode, Dr. Stewart. The second was an older man with a limp, and I can see from your faces that means something to you."

"Rhodes has a limp, from an old sporting injury, or so his aunt told me. Who was the later of the two to leave Taylor's?" Orlando knew what he wanted the answer to be.

"The man who was lame. Yet that's not all I have to say. This will particularly amuse Dr. Stewart. Angela Stafford doesn't have a twin sister, but she does have a cousin who resembles her closely and with whom she used to swap places when they were at school. And the cousin has no alibi for the night of Jardine's murder. Is that enough entities for you?"

"More than enough." Jonty groaned again. "I think she had that bloody cousin deliberately."

Chapter Nine

Ensconced in his own bed, Jonty didn't bother with either spectacles or book. He sat propped up on the pillows with a glass of wine in his hand. Mrs. Ward would kill him when she found out he'd been such a slut, but he was beyond caring, and his mind was racing. "Orlando, I need to talk to you."

"That sounds ominous. It's how I address the dunderheads when they make a total mess of things." Orlando produced a sly little grin. "Have you found out about my other man?"

"Idiot. Look, I want to get my head entirely clear vis-à-vis Taylor and his visitors, now that we've established the toings and froings at Dorking. A man with a limp—that has to be Rhodes. Please don't tell me that there's another lame man involved with this farrago."

"Just about every person of the male persuasion who has reached our notice is as hale as Apollo himself. Except that chap Rex and I refuse to believe he has anything to do with things. This is real life, not Conan Doyle. What about the other man who was seen near Taylor's house?"

"Well, his general description would fit Kermode, but it could also apply to about a half a million other blokes. It could even apply to Angela Stafford if she put on travesty."

"Eh?"

Jonty cuffed his lover's arm. "Your diction is appalling. What happened to 'Pardon me, Dr. Stewart'?"

"It died of a broken heart when all it got was a grunt in reply. Ow! That's twice you've thumped me tonight."

"It'll be more than that, the rate you're going. To return to *nos moutons*, travesty. Angela Stafford in her brother's britches, pretending to be a boy."

"It's a possibility, but she still doesn't have a motive…oh, you're joking aren't you?" For all that they'd known each other a year and a half, the number of times Orlando had been tricked must have exceeded a hundred. There still seemed to be a time delay to the part of his brain which registered that his leg was being pulled.

"Well I was, really. You're just so adorable when you allow yourself to be gulled." Jonty caressed his lover's cheek, letting his hand run down the angular lines of his jaw. "So we guess the man is Kermode." He frowned. "Except that he seems to have that dreaded thing, a genuine alibi for the murder of Taylor."

"How do you know? Why didn't you tell Wilson?"

"They'll find out soon enough if it's an inadequate one—I don't want to spoil their fun. It was Mrs. Ward who told me. She put two and two together when I was talking about Kermode—she really is a most astute woman—and did a little enquiring among her network of gossips and tittle-tattlers on her day off, the same day I went to Norwich. It seems that Mother Kermode and her little boy have been in London on and off these last few months, looking, or so they said, for suitable premises for their new business venture. They were in the capital when Jardine was killed, which we already knew, assuming we believe what the son said. They were also there the weekend that we were meeting the royals and Taylor was getting himself murdered. Mrs. W even established their whereabouts on that particular Sunday morning. The pair of them were in Brompton Oratory, enjoying the mass. Now that's not a million miles away from where Taylor lived."

"Could someone slip out from mass and rejoin it?"

"I have no idea. If the service was very busy, perhaps. It's not like St. Bride's chapel where you'd be hard pressed to scuttle out, it being small and everyone with their beady eyes darting about. I suppose if there were a throng…although there might be sidesmen in the offing. Anyway, it puts him close." Jonty put his arm round his lover, drew him down, manoeuvring to lie entwined together like a couple from one of Rubens' saucier ventures.

"Do you think Holmes and Watson have occasion to lie together like this?"

"Dr. Coppersmith, what an extraordinary question!" Trust Orlando to shatter the artistic fantasy with such an incongruous suggestion.

"Is it? When I read the stories I can't help but be struck by the degree of affection between them, stated and implied."

"That's a valid point, I'll grant you. I suspect, however, that Watson is far too much a ladies' man for anything romantic to be happening between them. It would be more like a brotherly affection on his part."

"And Holmes?" Orlando twisted around, nestled up into his lover's neck. "I sometimes identify with him, Jonty. It distresses me to think that he found no real love in his life."

"You old soppy pants." How could one man be so full of contrasts? Dr. Coppersmith—frightening to his students, fierce with his enemies, daft as a brush at times. "But you're quite right, you know. There's something dark and unhappy in Sherlock's soul that might just be linked up with denial of his true nature. If he loves his Watson and either can't manifest that love physically—he does strike me as being ascetic— or finds that love can't be reciprocated in anything other than friendship, it could drive any man to a seven per cent solution. Even you, had I come and stolen your chair then turned out to have a wife, a mistress and eleven children." Jonty stopped, slapped his lover's shoulder. "You're a genius. Simply brilliant."

"I know I am." Orlando grinned. "But what have I done to particularly deserve the soubriquet now?"

Jonty smiled. "I'll tell you afterwards."

"After what?"

"*Afterwards*." Jonty ran his hand down his lover's chest.

"You'll tell me now or there won't be any *before* to have an *afterwards* after. And don't laugh."

"I can't help it. Such mangled English, as awful as one of my dunderheads might produce in an essay on *As You Like It*. My genius boy. We've been looking at this case like the others we tackled, concentrating on revenge for yourself or a loved one, or a murder in order to cover up your misdemeanours. But what if it's about love, Orlando? About an unrequited devotion for someone which can't be manifest in contact with them? An affection which burns, tortures and eventually turns to violence?"

"Between?"

"Rhodes and Jardine. Or Rhodes and Taylor. Or both. What if my precious housemaster goaded those boys into using me because he felt a desire for one or other of them and wasn't capable of consummating it?"

Orlando thought a while, doodling on his lover's chest and fiddling with the hairs he found there. Jonty waited patiently, letting the immense brain grind small. "It could work, you know. He was obviously a lot closer to Jardine than he wanted to let on—you could tell that both from what he said and what he left unsaid. How about if Rhodes had grown jealous of the stream of men and women whom his lordship had bedded? He even knew all about the night callers. A touch of *if I can't have you, no one will.*"

"That's possible I suppose. Or what if he felt aggrieved that Jardine had, in effect, renounced him with this impending confession? You can be sure that he wouldn't have been left untainted by any public declaration."

Orlando closed his eyes, shuddering. "I wish you'd been there in Epsom—I was wrong not to take you. You'd have been able to pick out the lies from the half truths. And Rhodes lied about Taylor, I realise that fact now. That little toerag never had a crisis of conscience, not if your man Kermode is to be believed."

"We need to see Rhodes together, Orlando. Settle this matter once and for all, by which I don't just mean the murders. And soon, preferably before the police get to him."

"I know that. Tomorrow." Orlando favoured his lover's arm with the most gentle of kisses. It was time for *befores* and he wasn't going to turn his nose up at the offer. "We'll leave early and spend the night in London if need be."

"Very bold, very decisive. It's no wonder your old rugby chums saw such a change in you." Jonty wriggled into the crook of Orlando's arm and let his fingers start to doodle on the man's breasts. "They must have thought you a canny player. I wonder what they'd say if they knew how good you were at this sort of mauling."

"If you're going to start making obscene rugby jokes I'll go off to my own room, and won't that give Mrs. Ward a shock to find she has two beds to make in the morning?"

The threat was patently hollow as Orlando, far from showing any signs of departing, was starting to explore with his hands, surveying the hills and valleys of Jonty's well-developed frame.

"Not once will I mention ruck or tackle, not so long as you carry on doing that." Jonty shut his eyes, luxuriating in the sensations those mapmaking fingers were causing, as they traced their way ever downwards. He wondered whether Orlando kept that chart in his head, if he'd a clear diagram of every inch of his lover's body to which he could refer when they made love. Or did he tear up the map every time, begin the exploration afresh?

Orlando's lips were contributing to the construction of the atlas, too, plumbing the depths of Jonty's mouth, sounding the ridges of his ears and neck. It might be true that there were no new lands to be conquered here, no territory which hadn't already been claimed in the name of Coppersmith, but it didn't matter. The re-treading of old ground was never monotonous, not in their bed.

"Jonty." Orlando's voice, hoarse with passion, was barely more than a whisper. "I wish I was the only person to have journeyed here."

It wasn't the best choice of words. Jonty knew that his lover was referring to Richard Marsters, he'd done the same on past occasions, but the phrase carried other resonances now. The first explorers had been invaders, unwelcome and incapable of being resisted. He swallowed hard, trying to muster up some sort of courage—surely their bed couldn't witness another debacle? "So do I, with all my heart. Virgin territory for you to discover, like some Livingstone or Cook. We could always pretend."

"We could, one day. Not now, though. Not till this case is all cleared." Orlando's hands moved off in exploration once more, Jonty making a good front of willing them onwards, until they'd found their El Dorado. "Yes, that's it, just there. That's the source of all pleasure, if not the source of the Nile."

"Would you please give the clever talk a rest for once?" Orlando didn't even need to say he was tired of the analogies. "All I want is to *do our duty*." The usual phrase, their private idiom for "making love".

His hands went back to where they'd been—this time Jonty didn't say a word, although his own movements spoke volumes, making it plain that, again, there'd be no bodily union. He'd bring Orlando to a climax and let himself be taken to the same place, although the pleasure would be tinged with bitterness.

The soft moans Orlando spoke into the night were interspersed with other, harsher voices. *Stop it, Stewart. The more you fight the worse it'll be for both of us.* Words Jonty thought he'd forgotten, come back to taunt him. He held his lover closer; together, as ever, in rapture as in distress.

Jonty, spent, if not really satisfied, snuggled against his lover's chest. "It doesn't matter if other hands, other mouths have gone before you. Nobody has ever made me as happy as you do, Orlando. Orlando?"

A gentle snore gave him his answer. At other times it would have sounded as sweet as a sonnet—now it just reminded him how good he was becoming at pretending.

*

"Mr. Rhodes, will you tell us why you did it?"

Jonty's voice sounded clear as a bell in the neat study of the house on Epsom Downs. How they'd wangled themselves entry into the hallowed inner sanctum Orlando still wasn't sure, but old Miss Rhodes having taken a shine to them hadn't harmed matters. She'd fawned over Jonty, saying what a nice lad he was, how much he reminded her of someone she couldn't quite place.

"I don't understand what you're referring to." Sebastian Rhodes had been less keen to entertain them, yet it was better to be bearded in his own den rather than in front of the old lady.

"I think you do. Why did you make Jardine and Taylor do those things to me?"

Orlando tried to regain his composure. This wasn't what they'd agreed upon during the journey down to Epsom, not at all. The plan had been to gently probe Rhodes about the places where his story was inconsistent with what other people had said, to gradually winkle out the truth about his relationships with the other main players, to creep towards a confession of guilt.

But now Jonty was ploughing in with both fists—metaphorically for the moment, although that could become literally given the look on his face. His deep blue eyes were like cold sapphires and he bore the visage of some avenging angel, pure righteousness and retribution.

Orlando felt confused and not a little frightened. Last night, in bed, he'd been visited with awful dreams, reflections of the one question he'd tried hard to ignore—whether Rhodes had actually been smitten with a crush on Jonty himself. If that turned out to be the case, murder would definitely be back on his agenda and bare hands the only possible weapon.

Rhodes seemed just as stunned. "I'm still unsure what you mean..."

"Don't prevaricate, *Mr. Rhodes*." Jonty made the title seem like the worst sort of insult. "You can't play games with me any more."

There was a long awkward pause before the man replied. "I will not discuss this in front of *him*." Rhodes gave Orlando a look of pure hatred.

"Dr. Coppersmith." Jonty mustered a huge amount of tenderness into his voice. "Would you be so very kind as to step outside for a moment? I hope that this won't take too long."

"As you wish, Dr. Stewart." Orlando bowed to his friend, cast a withering glance at his enemy then left, although he hovered about outside the door, just in case he needed to leap in. Inspector Wilson was lurking out in the road with a muscular constable at his side, ready to make an arrest should it prove necessary, but that was a good hundred yards away. He eyed a stout ceremonial baton on the wall, then carefully plucked it down and kept it handy. *Just in case.*

"Will you take a seat, Stewart?"

The *Dr.* had been dropped, and it made Jonty think of how he'd been addressed back in the days when Rhodes could still scare the pants off him. Those days were long past. "You will sit down first and I'll decide whether to follow suit. Then you'll answer my question."

Rhodes eased into his chair, took a huge breath, composed himself. "It was a long time ago, Stewart."

"To me it feels as if it were yesterday. And always will, until I receive a proper explanation. Two of the men I could have gone to are dead and I'm fairly certain I know who killed them." Jonty carefully noted the pallor which spread over his enemy's face. "So I have to come to the third member of the triumvirate to demand the truth."

"Now, why do you define me as the third member? I never laid a hand on you—and before you say that because I know what happened I must be guilty, let me assure you Jardine and Taylor told me about what they'd done. And the contrition they felt."

Jonty snorted. "Your hands may not have been upon me but it was at your instigation it happened. Do they call it being an accessory before the fact?"

"And I ask again, why do you assume this?"

"Because I asked Taylor, when we saw him, and he confirmed all I'd suspected." Jonty could easily square the lie with his conscience, especially since a chance remark of Taylor's all those years ago had first implicated the housemaster.

Rhodes's eyebrows edged upwards. As the man steepled his hands, Jonty noticed that the fingers were trembling—this game was getting to its culmination. "Stewart, we both know Timothy Taylor wasn't the most honest of men. He lied to both of us, I suspect, about a number of things."

"I'm sure he did, but this wasn't one of his fabrications. We both know it was you who set Jardine upon me, and I'd like to know why. I'll sit here until you tell me." Jonty crossed his arms and legs, stared straight into his housemaster's eyes, confident that the man wouldn't keep the contact for long.

Rhodes leaned forward, laying his hands on the desk as if to steady himself. "You are quite right; I'll deny it no more. This has eaten into my conscience for years, now I must confess and find absolution. I beg you to understand that this was an aberration, the actions of a man who was at the time unwell. I abhor what I did then and I plead for your forgiveness. If I could go back and make what occurred at school disappear, never to have happened, I would."

He looked honest and truly contrite—Jonty wanted to take a poker to him. The fact that Rhodes had used almost the same words as Jonty himself had used to Orlando in a tender moment made it ten times worse.

"I'm sorry. I don't believe you. I don't believe you have an ounce of contrition in your soul."

"Dr. Stewart—" Jonty noticed the title had returned and was heartened to hear Rhodes trying to wheedle again, "—you are a Christian soul. Don't you believe that a sinner can repent?"

"I believe it implicitly, although I don't think it has happened this time. I'm prepared to accept that Christopher Jardine had a change of heart and wanted to make some sort of confession. I shouldn't be surprised if that contributed to his death. But in your case I don't see any evidence of a change of heart, not like there was with his lordship." Jonty spoke his suppositions as if they were established facts and the ploy seemed to be working. "Did *you* once try to contact me, or Simon Kermode, or the family of that poor lad who committed suicide?"

Rhodes's face turned a deathly colour—he had to steady himself again on the desk. "Andrew Nicholls didn't commit suicide, it was a terrible accident." For the first time, the man's voice sounded tremulous.

"If that's what you seek to believe, then so be it. I know the truth. I know exactly what happened." Jonty wasn't sure where the words he was speaking came from, although he was certain he should be saying them. "But I want to hear why, from your own lips."

"Can I help you, dear?" Auntie appeared around the corner, smiling sweetly and seeming not to notice the blunt instrument which Orlando was trying to hide behind his back.

"No, thank you. I'm just waiting for my friend. He and Mr. Rhodes have confidential matters to discuss."

"Old pupil, is he?" Auntie beamed. "Sebastian is awfully fond of helping out his former scholars. They'll probably be chin-wagging for ages. Would you like some tea?"

"That's very kind, but I'm replete, thank you."

"Oh that's a shame, I thought that you might like to come and look with me at some old photographs I was sorting through. There's a few from Sebastian's time as housemaster. Your friend may be on them."

Orlando felt torn. He knew he should stay at the door, yet what the old lady said was piquing his interest. "I'm sure they're charming..."

"Oh, they are. There are some particularly nice ones of Sebastian with one of the pupils who came and stayed here. So sad—the young man died not long afterwards in a tragic accident."

Orlando started, regained himself, patted the lady's arm. "Miss Rhodes, I think that I would love to see those photographs."

Auntie produced seemingly interminable group shots from school, in which, if Jonty did feature, he was no more than a fuzzy presence, unrecognisable to his lover. At last they reached the ones Orlando found really interesting, a set of photos which Auntie displayed with particular pride, ones taken at her house and featuring her nephew and a handsome blond youth. Miss Rhodes carefully explained that these had been taken in the summer holidays some years ago, although she couldn't recall how many. The boy had been in St. Vincent house at school and had come to stay for a fortnight while his parents were travelling.

"Such lovely manners he had. I do admire comportment in a man." Auntie beamed at her guest, to whom she'd clearly taken quite a shine.

Orlando wondered why women of a certain age seemed to want to ply him with tea, cakes and confidences. "You said he had some sort of an accident?"

"Indeed, in the autumn term, not long after he stayed here. Sebastian visited me a fortnight after that, when I'd been very unwell and he was given leave to come here for a few days. He told me all about it. It seems this boy—I really wish I could remember his name—fell on a knife and it entered his neck." Orlando winced at the memories this evoked but managed to hide it. "Sebastian was so upset. He cried like a baby when he told me."

Orlando patted Auntie's hand and studied the pictures again—this same young man appeared in the photograph on Rhodes's desk. Perhaps he was reading too much into these other prints, seeing what he wanted to, but he noticed a distinct air of unease about the boy. As if he profoundly wished to be elsewhere, while Rhodes appeared to be a man enraptured. In one portrait the look he was giving his pupil seemed undeniable. It was identical to the one that Orlando was giving Jonty in the photograph which graced his own wall.

Orlando's mind raced, as if he could influence what was going on in Rhodes's study by sheer willpower or by divine intervention. As he'd done before, when things had been too difficult, he prayed to the God in whom he'd no belief. *He says that You talk to him, then speak to him now. Tell him to ask about the boy who committed suicide.*

Jonty hadn't given up the verbal assault, even in the face of repeated denials from his adversary. "So why did he cut his own jugular, this Nicholls? Was it that he couldn't face the pain any more, the bleeding and the discharge?" He saw Rhodes blanch, ignored it. "Or was it the shame, the sense of being treated as nothing more than a lump of meat? Or was it simply that he couldn't go through another twenty-four hours of thinking *is tonight the night, again?*"

"I have told you, Dr. Stewart, Andrew Nicholls did not take his own life." Even Rhodes didn't sound as if he believed it.

"What I'd like to know is who you set on him. It couldn't have been Taylor or Jardine. Who did your dirty work then?"

Rhodes smote the desk with his fist. "Do you think that I would let any other hands touch Andrew Nicholls' flesh?"

Stewart sneered, "Kept him all to yourself then, did you? No wonder he topped himself if he'd had your paws all over him."

Rhodes rose, looking as if he was about to pick up the paperweight and launch it. "You will take every word of that back, Dr. Stewart. I loved Andrew Nicholls."

If Jonty felt the case turning upside down again, as it had done half a dozen times these last few weeks, he tried hard not to show it. He had Rhodes on the back foot and wanted to keep him there. "And he hated you in return, as all your victims did? So much that he had to take his own life?"

"You don't understand." Rhodes crumpled, sat again, looked a broken man. "He did love me, he just didn't realise it. He was too weighed down with conventions and the expectations of those around him. They wouldn't let him love me."

Jonty shook his head, nauseous at the self-delusion. "So, because he wouldn't let you lay your filthy hands on him, you took it out on Kermode, and on me?" A sudden thought struck him. "Kermode has the same colouring and build as I do. Did Nicholls? Was it like having him back at the school? Did you watch Jardine having his way with me and pretend it was you and him?" He suddenly registered the gilt framed photograph which stood on the desk. "Is this him? This poor, benighted-looking lad?"

Rhodes had his head in his hands, overwhelmed by Jonty's last onslaught. "I would never have harmed Andrew. He didn't understand what love was about. I tried to show him, I..." He stopped, abruptly, looked up. "I have nothing more to say to you."

It was a last effort at wresting control of the interview, but the avenging angel was having none of it.

He wouldn't spare this city even for fifty righteous men.

"So you killed the thing you loved, as surely as if you'd wielded the knife yourself. And because you loved him so very much, this poor lad, years later you had to kill the man who was threatening to expose you. You heard what Jardine said to Kermode, how he was sorry and wanted to make a clean breast of things, and were so concerned to protect your 'love' that you took up a poker and effectively put an end to all the danger."

"He wanted to go back to the school, to that wretch of a new Headmaster—the one who hates me and wants to destroy all I hold sacred. His plan was to get Barrington to contact you and that other boy, what's-his-name, to make some sort of act of contrition. Then he wanted the school to find out whether anything similar has gone on in the past, in St. Vincent's. In *my* house. Jardine said that Andrew had taken his own life. I couldn't listen to such lies, nor would I have them spoken to Barrington—he would soon contrive evidence to support such slander. So I killed him." Rhodes looked at the photograph on his desk, at Jonty, at the picture of Nicholls again. "I couldn't have him saying such things."

Jonty fought hard not to feel sorry for this man. Years of hatred and fear were dissolving into scorn and then something akin to pity. "And Taylor? He had to suffer the same fate for the same reason?"

It took Rhodes an age to drag his gaze away from the beloved face in the frame. When he did, he wore a beatific expression. "Taylor? Oh yes, I killed him too."

Chapter Ten

"Matthew. What on earth are you doing here?" Charing Cross station seemed awash with young men, but not so many that Jonty couldn't spot a familiar face. On their platform, to boot.

"Off to stay with your mother. Did she neglect to tell you?"

"She did just that." Jonty was happy enough at the surprise. "The old girl keeping secrets from us, eh, Dr. Coppersmith?"

Orlando wore such a look of disappointment, albeit fleeting and covered with a forced smile, that Matthew felt obliged to make some sort of explanation. "We met at a mutual acquaintance's house in London. When Mrs. Stewart discovered I was the man you met on Jersey, she insisted I be her guest for the Easter weekend."

"Quite right, too. Couldn't think of better company. Dr. Coppersmith, could you check that the trunks are stowed properly? That porter had a fey look in his eye." They watched Orlando along the platform. "Please excuse *someone's* bad humour. He's no doubt cross that we won't be the only guests and probably miffed to only discover the fact at Charing Cross station. No, don't apologise." He raised his hand, smiling sweetly. "It'll do him good to realise that Mama has other friends and that he can't always be the favoured one. He'll soon see sense—it'll be an appropriate end to this investigation, for one thing."

"I'm looking forward to hearing all the detail." Matthew fought to keep his voice level. "And I am immensely grateful, as you know."

Jonty slapped him on the shoulder, leaving any words for now—they both knew how much this case meant.

They'd boarded and relative calm had descended onto their first-class carriage when they discovered that Mrs. Stewart had lined up another surprise. It came in the form of the fourth man who bounced through the door just as the train was about to depart, Rex Prefontaine, his limp not inhibiting a spectacular leap from platform to carriage.

From the very start in that bumpy train compartment the four men rubbed along together well, even Orlando coming out of his bad temper by the time they'd passed Reigate.

"I was so relieved to hear Rhodes had been arrested." Matthew was about to carry on, express his true gratitude, as Rex's intrigued expression brought him up short. Why on earth was he baring his soul in the presence of a stranger? "I'm sorry, Mr. Prefontaine, we'll keep our business for later."

"As you see fit, Mr. Ainslie." Rex inclined his head to one side—a sweet, endearing gesture. "If it can't keep, I can be remarkably good at being deaf, or so my mother assures me."

Matthew was tempted to return to the Jardine case, to relate how Angela Stafford had been all floods of tears and thankfulness when he'd told her the news. How, although barely coherent with joy, she'd apologised that she and her brother would be spending some time with family abroad and would Ainslie be very upset if he didn't come and give his thanks in person just yet? He caught the warning look in Jonty's eye and turned the subject to horseracing.

It had been just a matter of days since Rhodes's arrest, yet all these events already seemed ages ago, receding further into the past as the train moved deeper into Sussex and the rather unreal world of the Stewarts' estate. Perhaps when they were there, the whole case would seem like some strange dream, of which the only tangible evidence would be a new suit, new socks, and Jonty's not having to keep part of his life hidden from the people he loved. The four men took the Stewart carriage from the station to the Old Manor, Rex's and Matthew's eyes popping out like organ stops as they rounded the bend in the road which opened up a proper view of the Stewart house.

"I had no idea, Jonty," Matthew was struggling to find his breath, let alone the right words, "when your mother invited us down, that I'd be staying in a castle. 'Our little country house', she described it as."

"You have to be very careful with Mama. She tends to hide the family lights under a bushel and to rather underestimate the size of things. She bewailed the small size of the Christmas goose last December then the thing turned out to be about as big as an ostrich. And she's convinced that I'm thin and in need of a good feed."

Rex grinned. "My mother's just the same. Fusses and frets over me as if I were only nine years old. Does she ask you if you're still wearing your undershirt, even when it's eighty degrees outside?"

"She does indeed. She even sent me to my bed last winter for being out without my hat on. I love her dearly, Mr. Prefontaine, but she would try the patience of a saint. And tell him off for his halo not being on straight."

They pulled in through the gateway, where Richard Stewart greeted them. He sometimes watched from one of the upper bedrooms then sneaked down to be first to meet guests, determined to steal a march on his wife. Helena Stewart soon followed, dressed in as much finery as if she'd been summoned to see Queen Alexandra. Her son and his lover might have warranted her grey silk, but the other young men deserved the sapphire blue which matched her eyes.

She beamed brightly at all and sundry then grabbed Orlando for a fierce embrace while Mr. Stewart shook his son's hand heartily. If Matthew was worried that his hostess had it in mind to give him a cuddle as well, he'd underestimated her sense of propriety.

"Mr. Ainslie, I'm so pleased that you were able to join us. And Mr. Prefontaine, it is my honour to have you at my table." She let them kiss her hand, then turned to Jonty. "Not looking as thin as usual, dear. That Mrs. Ward must be doing a good job." She squeezed Stewart junior as if he were a cloth to be wrung out, then gathered her guests together for tea and cakes to recompense them for the mighty tribulations of the train journey from the capital.

"You've taken a bit of a shine to Mr. Prefontaine," Jonty whispered to his mother as they made their way to the drawing room. "Should Papa be worried?"

Mrs. Stewart slapped her son's backside. "Behave yourself, child. Your father and I both admire the type of person who's determined to make his own way in the world, especially when it's against a background of 'Old Money'. Too easy for youngsters to take it all for granted." She didn't make reference to the man's marked limp nor did she speculate as to how it had come about, which showed great strength of character on her part. "How are you?" It wasn't just a pleasantry, mother to son. When she'd heard of Rhodes's confession Mrs. Stewart had cried, sobbing down the phone and getting herself into an awful tizzy, cursing the housemaster and praising her two boys almost in the same breath.

"Much better. How's Papa?" Mr. Stewart had been noble and gallant, glad to have played a small part in bringing a double murderer to justice.

"He's starched his upper lip again." Mrs. Stewart winked—she'd already confessed to her beloved sprog that his father had burst into tears the minute he'd put the earpiece on the telephone stand after hearing the news.

"Daft old thing. I do love you both. And I'm so immensely relieved."

Not relieved enough to have broken the bedroom moratorium, though. Jonty and Orlando were given their usual set of rooms, in the guest wing the far side of the gatehouse, with the oddly accented footman, Macgregor, to dance attendance on them, but very little in the way of hanky-panky was going to be gracing the huge four-poster beds. Orlando had hoped Rhodes's confession was going to prove the turning point, the solution of the case the catalyst for a triumphal recommencement of intimacy. It wasn't. Jonty showed even less interest in 'doing his duty' and wouldn't even discuss why, more than saying, "There's pieces of the jigsaw still missing and I'm not even sure what picture I'm trying to make any more."

Orlando hoped that the Old Manor would work its magic, as it had on his broken memory. He wasn't even bothered that Matthew was located at the bottom of their staircase—the man could camp outside their doors, for all Orlando cared, so long as Jonty got over whatever was inhibiting him.

Matthew's suite was rather darker than some of the other rooms, although very atmospheric. He'd been offered a choice of this or something in the main wing, but he said he'd plumped for the sensation of being in a real castle, not the modern comfort of the apartments above the library.

Rex was given a ground floor suite directly off the gatehouse, just the other side of where the portcullis might have been had the original owner of the castle not run out of money, honour, and his head before his plans could come to fruition. He had his own bathroom and sitting room, which wasn't afforded to the others, who had their sleeping and living apartments combined. Mrs. Stewart insisted that it was because of his status as a foreign national—the stranger in our land and all that—although everyone knew he'd been given this suite to avoid his having to limp up and down the unforgiving stone staircases.

The other Stewart children had commitments with their own families or in-laws over Easter week, so Mrs. Stewart had just a small, exclusive male party to fuss over. She didn't miss the presence of her kind, always having averred she was a man's woman, totally happy to retire alone after the coffee and await her guests in splendid isolation. Her reaction to Orlando's appearance in his new suit proved a mixture of pride and admiration, squeezing his cheeks then making him turn around a dozen times for *everyone*, an everyone consisting at the time of her and Jonty, to admire it.

Over the next three days, the men spent hours playing croquet in the early spring sunshine, attending the necessary services in church or concentrating at bridge after dinner, usually letting their host take one of the hands while whoever sat out chatted with their hostess. They avoided tennis, not just because it seemed unfair to Rex and his leg—Orlando still couldn't quite dissociate in his mind tennis, Matthew Ainslie, and unnecessary liberties. On the odd occasion when rain had threatened they'd entertained themselves with billiards or snooker. They barely touched on the Alistair Stafford case, even though Jonty kept hinting that he felt one of his missing pieces was wrapped up in it. Here, in an unreal world of English delights, it could wait for its full denouement to be expounded.

The library, Easter Saturday, saw five men playing a hand of cards after lunch and the conversation turning to literary matters. Mr. Stewart turned it to murder mysteries, singing the praises of Doyle and Collins. Matthew sat contentedly listening to the conversation, chipping in with the expert viewpoint of the successful publisher. Rex was astounding everyone by saying how much he'd enjoyed "The Story of a Fierce Bad Rabbit" when a stifled snort emerged from behind *The Times*.

Jonty slapped the person who was reading it. "You'll excuse Orlando, he's an Oxford man originally and we still haven't knocked all the stupidity and rudeness out of him."

Rex inclined his head. "You should see the college rivalries we have at home. Makes Oxford against Cambridge look like 'The Story of Miss Moppet'."

"You need to see the varsity rugby match, Rex—less Beatrix Potter than something out of the Old Testament. Samson himself would have quailed to see some of the forwards I've had to face, even if he'd had his ass's jawbone to hand."

"I understand the cricket's like that, too." Rex's eyes lit up. "A veritable case of smiting them 'hip and thigh'."

Everyone appreciated the joke—this was as quick as any wit the Stewarts usually displayed.

"Touché, Mr. Prefontaine." Mr. Stewart rose, bowed and doffed an imaginary cap. "I know that my wife has an excellent eye for a guest and she hasn't disappointed us so far. One day I'll take you to Lord's and you can see if any of the England bowlers match up to Delilah's boyfriend."

"Talking of Delilah, Papa, are the rector and his family coming to dinner on Monday?" The living of the parish was in the gift of the Stewarts and, while the present incumbent had been chosen for his true Christian qualities, his wife was still on probation. He had a sister of perhaps thirty, whose marital prospects were scuppered by a lack of both suitable introductions and reasonable dowry. Mrs. Stewart was a sight too keen to try and play matchmaker for her, and Jonty had an awful feeling she was lining up Matthew or Rex as potential altar fodder.

"Not this year. They have another invitation, which might be as well." Mr. Stewart cast a small sideways glance at his guests, a glance that his son acknowledged with a wink.

"I rather think that…" No one found out what Orlando thought, the butler interrupting with an announcement that tea was served. And such a tea it proved, marked by huge quantities of exquisite pastries and cakes, with a side helping of faux pas.

"Mr. Prefontaine," Mrs. Stewart inquired, smiling, "I do so worry about that leg of yours. I was watching you all strolling down to the village and I couldn't help wonder how it happened. Have you always had a problem with it?"

To everyone's immense relief he simply beamed at his hostess and tapped the offending limb. "I'm so pleased you asked. People never do, you know, they just try to guess. It's no secret. I was out riding, took a fence, or perhaps I should say I tried to take the fence, but the horse had different ideas. She and I had a distinct parting of the ways, meaning my poor leg had an altercation with a tree trunk. It came off the worse and the doctors could do nothing for it. It might have been poetic justice if they could have used that tree to make me a false limb, except they reckoned it was the wrong sort of wood. So here I am like Captain Ahab from the left knee down and only a mountain ash to blame, not a white whale." He began to laugh.

Matthew smiled affectionately at this brave young man. "Was it long ago?"

"When I was eighteen, although I won't say how many years back that was. It was truly a blessing in disguise. For two years I couldn't be made to dance with debutantes or cousins or any other annoying young women. I could get on with my studies, play cards and fish. What more could a man want?"

Mrs. Stewart remembered, aloud, what her beloved Jane Austen had said about a single man in possession of a good fortune and what he must be in want of. Luckily she didn't then go on to draw a parallel between Elizabeth Bennett and any young ladies in the vicinity of the Old Manor, being hastily distracted by her husband.

"Tell Orlando about how your charity is getting on."

Mrs. Stewart beamed, launching into a lengthy description of the work her foundation did with 'unfortunate young girls'. "We help them learn to be nursery maids or cooks within reputable houses or teachers in church schools, earning themselves a good reference in the process. It's rewarding to furnish these lasses with a decent future and a reputable past at the same time. Although we always need money to help provide for them when they first set out into the respectable world. I wonder whether any of you gentlemen would like to help?" She turned to Matthew. "You look like the sort of young man who'd appreciate a fallen woman."

Jonty bit his lip. He pinched his leg. He thought about the back of his neck, anything to try to stop laughing. He would have succeeded had he not caught Rex's eye—the man was clearly in the same situation. It was no use, they both exploded into laughter at the same time, Mr. Stewart joining in as well and the giggles spreading through the company.

"Mama," Jonty wheezed. "You've excelled yourself there."

"I think I rather have. Mr. Ainslie, will you ever forgive me? I meant to cast no aspersions on your character."

"Ma'am, there is nothing to apologise for or forgive. I haven't laughed so much in years, truly. This has been an Easter without comparison for me and I'm honoured to have shared it with you all."

"Such a gracious speech, young man, I do appreciate it. You really must teach my youngest son some of your charming manners. This calls for champagne, the very best we can rouse out, Richard."

It arrived, it proved magnificent and they drank many a toast. Supper was a simple meal and the party took to the drawing room earlier than normal. At last the Stafford case got the discussion it had been due, the warm glow of champagne and port loosening tongues all round.

They explained the background and details patiently to Rex, everyone chipping in at odd times and confusing the poor chap to the extent he had to get out his handkerchief and make a sign of surrender.

"I'm more confused now than when I tried to read Chaucer in his original form. Orlando, would you do the honours and tell me the story simply, like Miss Potter does?"

Orlando rose to the challenge, one no harder than drumming algebra into even the most obtuse of his students. He bowdlerised the link between Matthew and Alistair Stafford then skirted round the connections between the victims, the culprit and the Stewart family. It was all presented in terms of the honour of the old school—if this astute young man subsequently put two and two together, they weren't going to help him with his addition.

The discussion ranged over the detective processes used, the road towards denouement, and Rhodes's repeated words on and, according to the police, after arrest. *Do what you will with me in regards to the murders, only let everyone know that Andrew Nicholls did not commit suicide. He's innocent of everything.* Rex listened, eyes aglow with the puzzle laid before him and quickly coming to the nub of the case.

"So you reckon that Taylor saw Rhodes in between your two meetings and somehow that gave him a bit more pep when he faced you again? Then his confidante turned on him and gave him what for. Makes a lot of sense."

"That's how the police see it." Jonty felt troubled, a small knot of doubt in his stomach. Missing pieces of the jigsaw—there'd be no peace until he had every one of them in place. "I'm sure there'd been some contact before that. It wouldn't surprise me if Taylor believed we'd been put onto him that first time, to beat him up or something. He was more frightened than he had any right to be. Anyway, while I'm fairly certain that Rhodes killed Jardine, the more I think on it, the more I'm unsure about Taylor. I'd love to see my housemaster hang for a double killing—and I appreciate that's not at all a Christian attitude—but I just don't see why he should kill Taylor. Strikes me they'd have been on the same side, and the man posed no risk to the precious memory of Andrew Nicholls."

Rex looked out the window, a habit they'd all noticed he adopted when he was deep in thought. "Yet he admitted to the crime."

"He did, but it was peculiar, the words he used when he confessed, and I've been over it an awful lot in my mind since then. I even wondered whether he couldn't actually remember whether he'd done the deed or not. You know, showing early signs of the same memory loss which affects his aunt at times. But he seemed too much in possession of his faculties for that." Jonty's fingers drummed on the chair arm, a tattoo of doubt and unease.

"And the police said he was the second person to visit Taylor that morning?" Rex kept his eye fixed on the grounds.

"Assuming that he was the man with the limp, and we have no real reason to doubt that, yes." Jonty was adamant about this—he'd have no other lame men admitted into the case. Except Rex, who was proving a notable bloodhound.

"So if Rhodes didn't kill Taylor, did a third person come along or do you think he was already dead when your old housemaster got there?"

Jonty nodded, schoolboy enthusiasm lighting up his face. "That's what we've recently concluded, haven't we, Orlando?"

"Jonty, who's known in police circles as the man who doubts all alibis, has convinced himself that Simon Kermode wasn't actually at mass. He was making his way to see Taylor, whose head he smacked in, then returned to his mother, who's covering for him. Dr. Stewart made that theory up all from his own little bonce."

"Well it makes perfect sense, doesn't it? Matthew, don't you agree?" Jonty took his appeal to Caesar.

Matthew started out of deep concentration. "Sorry, Jonty, I was just piecing it all together. Your theory makes more sense than Rhodes killing him, but the question remains. Why did the man then admit to it?"

Rex's handsome face puckered into a grin. "I had a friend who always owned up to all the naughty things that had gone on. He'd be punished and then the culprit would be shamed into owning up and my pal would be treated like a king for his altruism. He said that being locked in his room was small beer compared to all the treats he got afterwards. Until his mother got wise, that is."

And all further chance of speculation as to whether this could apply to Rhodes ended as Mrs. Stewart decided that all the talk was going round in circles and made them go out and get some fresh air, "like sensible lads".

Chapter Eleven

Easter Sunday dawned bright and clear. The rain had left a sheen on everything which the dazzling spring sunshine highlighted, giving it a clarity that was breathtaking. Orlando prepared for church with more enthusiasm than normal—the Old Manor hadn't worked any magic on Jonty's reticence in bed, but maybe Easter communion would. The great festivals in the church year always affected him, infusing him with a joy which almost shone in his face. Joy and peace were what he needed more than ever.

Jonty rose from confession and absolution with the façade of high spirits firmly in place and the signs of gnawing pain still there for anyone who knew him well enough to recognise them. He seemed particularly pensive during the readings and even the huge meal which followed their return from church, a piece of roast beef about the size of Hertfordshire with more Yorkshire pudding than would sink a battleship, didn't entirely break him from his thoughts. There was one last thing to try.

The Tudor walled garden at the back of the library was Jonty's favourite haunt. As a boy he'd escaped from his brothers there, hiding in a nook he'd discovered amongst the stems of an old vine, or had taken his books out onto the lawn to read and dream. He'd loved it ever since, regarding it as a magical place, the portals of which once crossed would lead the wanderer into another time and place. He could even convince himself that he'd been transported back to the time when the garden was newly planted, or perhaps when it'd been left to become overgrown, a time when even the Bard himself might have been encountered wandering among the lavender beds and caressing the roses.

He'd taken Orlando there, the first time they'd visited the house, back in the previous August, showing him the lavender walks, where their senses had been assaulted by the vivid hues, lavish scents and the incessant humming of the bees among the flowers. A "bee-loud glade" it had certainly been. Jonty believed the garden was at its best in spring, when the clarity of the blue sky was unparalleled at any other time of the year, or in the autumn when the moist smell of the earth and grass filled the nose with delight, but Orlando vowed that summer had to be the most lovely time in that most lovely of places.

It felt almost like summer when the four men wandered into it, a bright, warm spring Sunday afternoon with just the type of azure sky which Jonty said was perfect for the setting. They found the lavender walks, too early in the year for any but the most adventurous of bees, but still sweet smelling and sensuous. They rubbed the leaves of the shrubs, drank in the heady scents, immersed themselves in their surroundings. Orlando had a chess set and board under his arm, to set up on his favourite bench by the old wall or in the summer house. Thrashing his lover at chess had become about the closest they got to intimacy these last few weeks—he'd have been closer tackling Jonty out on the St. Bride's pitches.

A strange moaning noise broke their quiet pleasure, a sound which grew louder and closer, revealing itself as coming from a cat whose coat could only be described as near to blue as grey could ever legitimately reach. A lean, handsome creature with a leonine gait and gaze.

Matthew knelt down on his haunches, rubbing the animal's chin and back, cooing to it gently.

"You like cats, Matthew?" Rex looked down fondly too, although Orlando couldn't tell if the affectionate gaze was directed at the well-groomed animal or the well-groomed man who was making such a fuss of him. Matthew certainly looked twice the man he'd appeared ever since they met him. If only some of that happiness would rub off on Jonty.

"I'm fond of felines of any type, from the smallest kitten to the lions in the zoological gardens. This little chap reminds me much more of the latter than the former."

"I always said you had a lot of sense. This isn't just any moggy, you know."

The men made their way to the summer house, a building perfectly placed to enjoy the sunshine at this time of year and its corresponding point in the autumn. Their new friend decided to follow, making his low growl as he went, weaving in and out of four sets of footsteps with alacrity, avoiding being trodden on and slinking his tail along legs and calves. He was happily tolerated.

As they sat on the pleasant wooden bench, sharing some of Rex's cigarettes from his elegant golden case, and setting out the chess pieces, the cat stretched himself along their feet and waited to be adored. In due course he inevitably was, Jonty caressing the backs of his ears until the creature showed signs of dozing.

"Do you keep a cat, Matthew?" Rex let the smoke drift lazily from his nostrils.

"No one really *keeps* a cat, do they? Quite the opposite."

"That's certainly true in this case." Jonty seemed as if he was going to enlighten them, but Orlando wanted the game to start. It became apparent that their feline friend wasn't able to enjoy his sleep. Ears and paws twitched, till at last his head rose to eye a forsythia bush from which a raucous twittering was emerging.

"Something's annoying this little guy." Rex smiled and smoothed the soft fur of the cat's back. "Don't get so het up, puss. It's only a bird, not worth your worrying about."

Matthew smiled too, his face a picture of delight. "It's some ignorant robin in the depths of that bush. It doesn't realise that he's keeping the king of the jungle from his rightful slumbers."

The king soon decided that he would put up with very little more. Rising and stretching, he fixed the shrubbery with a cool green eye and set off in search of prey, leaving his worshippers to listen for the robin's demise.

"You should come and see my home, Matthew. The fall would be the best time."

"Fall, Rex? I don't follow you."

"I'm sorry—the autumn you'd call it. The colours are certainly spectacular then. You would see us at our very best." He smiled, thoughts far away. "I was thinking of my family home. There are groves of trees my ancestors planted purposely to set off each other's finery when the leaves take on their loveliest hues. Trees they didn't necessarily see to maturity, but which they've left as a living legacy, as this garden's been left to be enjoyed by later generations."

"I'm afraid that the autumn is our busiest time. Summer's when I take my holidays."

"That's when we met," Orlando piped up, immediately regretting it. They didn't want to be touching on murder here, not now there was the hint of a genuinely happy smile on Jonty's face.

Rex barely acknowledged that he'd spoken. "Come in the summer then, Matthew. We have a private beach and moorings—you could swim to your heart's content, with no one to bother you. And we could sail out to the islands, watch the whales. I bet you've never seen one of those." Rex's face lit up. "Blue seas and skies that seem to melt into one at the horizon, I miss it so much, even in this paradise."

"It would be my great delight." Matthew's words sounded as if they'd caught in his throat. "I fear, however, that what with the voyage there and back I couldn't afford the time away from work."

"Nonsense! Your business is in excellent shape. It's been improving year on year from what I've heard, and you've got excellent men working for you. They could easily let you take a well-deserved rest. From what you and your friends have said, you hardly had a restful vacation last year. Make it a better one this." Rex's blue eyes glowed with merriment.

"How did you get to know so much about my business and the competency of my staff?"

Orlando wondered about that, too. He could see little beads of sweat breaking out above Matthew's collar, and the sun wasn't warm enough to cause them.

"Ah, I've been doing a little investigating." Rex grinned. "There's great potential in the printing business, Matthew, you know that as well as I do. It's a market that's going to grow—if we can pool our resources and those of our authors, we could make huge inroads both sides of the Atlantic. I've been looking for an English business to link mine with and yours would be ideal."

"You're suggesting some sort of joint venture?"

"I have some very definite proposals to put to you." Rex laid a hand on Matthew's arm. "I refuse to discuss it here, not just in deference to our eminent hostess who seems to have banned all talk of business, but because of my own fancy. Come to America and I'll talk to you then, about any proposal you have."

A quality in Rex's tone made Orlando glance up at Jonty. The man was trying hard to hide an impish grin—their eyes caught and a spark of something leapt between them. Not lust, not yet, but some quality within Jonty had changed and Orlando was jiggered if he knew why. They both looked across at the other two men, who seemed totally oblivious.

"Any proposal?"

"Absolutely any suggestions you have to make I'll consider most favourably..." Rex began to lean in, closing the transatlantic gap, but a third pair of lovebirds had appeared, in the form of Jonty's parents, with the butler behind them, bearing tea.

"That's a handsome cat you have here, Mrs. Stewart." Matthew accepted his tea, the delicate china cup looking like it might disintegrate in his rather clumsy hand.

"That tabby which the kitchen keeps? Only good for mousing, I've always thought."

"No, this was a smoky grey one, he was here a minute ago."

Mr. Stewart's ears pricked up, like a greyhound coursing a hare. "Lovely coat, had he? Made a strange growling noise as he walked along?"

"That's the very one," Rex averred. "What do you call him?"

"He doesn't have a name." Their host had a faraway look in his eye which was rather unnerving. Richard Stewart always seemed so very down to earth, this expression wasn't like him at all. "Never had one as far as I know, not even when I was a boy."

"I think I'm being rather dense here, Mr. Stewart." Matthew shook his head. "I mustn't have made it plain that I was referring to a cat which we saw here today, not the one that's in the portrait of your father." If he thought he was addressing someone losing their rational faculties he was too polite to show it.

"Ah. Yes. He wangled his way into that one, too. My father was very fond of him."

Mrs. Stewart couldn't ignore the puzzled looks on her guests' faces. "I believe an explanation is called for. Richard has a rather peculiar theory about that cat. I don't believe it for a moment."

The man in question smiled beatifically. "It is my profound belief that same cat has been in occupation of this castle ever since it was built."

The hush which fell on the company was so profound they couldn't just hear a pin drop, they would have heard its progress through the air. A bee buzzing through sounded like an underground train.

"You must explain exactly why we've come to that conclusion, Papa." Jonty bore his dreamy, contented look again.

"There is a grey cat—a peculiar smoky grey—which features in a story dating from the founding of this building. He appeared one day as the foundations were being laid and soon became a favourite of the masons, who spoiled him rotten, even when he walked through the mortar or got his little wet nose into things he shouldn't have." Mr. Stewart grinned in the same way as he did when he played with his grandchildren. A noble, upright, fiercely intelligent man, he was surprisingly childlike and sentimental when the occasion required.

His wife rolled her eyes. "I'm sure there was, dear, but as I've said on innumerable occasions, he was probably the founder of a great dynasty of moggies who've lived around here ever since, haunting the outbuildings and living on shrews."

"If that were so then we'd see the rest of the brood, mother cat and all the wretched little kittens. We'd be overrun by the things, yet we're not. All we see is a beautiful fully grown Tom who never changes from one generation to the next. He's in at least two of the portraits and it's patently obvious that it's the same creature."

"Now I'm the one who's confused." Rex's handsome face bore more than one wrinkle of contemplation. "I thought you said that your family only bought this place a few generations back?"

"We did, but we bought some of the paintings with it. One of them dates from just before we took this place over and shows the then-owner standing with my feline friend among the ruins. It really was a mess here, Mr. Prefontaine—why he should have wanted to preserve himself for posterity among the shambles he'd let the place fall into, I do not know. My father decided to emulate the picture by portraying himself alongside a building now restored to its original glory, or what would have been its glory had the founder not found himself headless and hopeless." Stewart senior grinned.

"Could it be that the family of cats live elsewhere? In the village or on one of the neighbouring farms?" Orlando sought for a prosaic explanation.

"Ah now, that's something which I feel is very difficult to account for." Jonty's eyes shone brightly. "I've known that cat since I was a lad. I've heard him, when he's in residence, wandering around the court at the best part of midnight. Then he's back at seven o'clock the next morning and this goes on for days on end. No owner would be likely to settle for that arrangement. And he's far too nicely groomed to be a feral moggy. His fur's as well kept as the most highfaluting pedigree and he doesn't ever look as if he's gone short of food."

"You never see him outside the walls, either." Mr. Stewart, eyes alive with enthusiasm, warmed to the subject of his little feline pal. "There's fine evenings I've been out looking at the bats or the stars, and you can hear him growling away inside the garden, but he never strays outside. I'll warrant he'd disappear once he passed outside the old boundaries."

"You think he's a spectre of some sort?" Orlando had been racking his brains. "I've been here on three occasions and in the Tudor garden each time, yet I've never seen him before."

Jonty sniggered. "You'd be far beneath his notice, Orlando. He has no time for mathematicians, being a cat with artistic tendencies. They say that Shakespeare's players put on a performance of *The Merchant of Venice* here and the Bard wrote the bit about 'a harmless necessary cat' at the last minute in honour of the little grey ball of fur. They also say that our feline friend calmly walked across the stage in the middle of Portia's big speech. Ow!" Jonty began to rub his leg, having forgotten what an iron hand his mother possessed.

"You will excuse my youngest son. He has a penchant for tall tales—I have no idea where he gets it from." Mrs. Stewart looked daggers at two of her three most beloved males. "The Bard was never here and if he was, that stupid cat would have felt the toe of his boot."

"The truth is that cat has no rhyme or reason to it. He's said to be the presager of good fortune and bring happiness to the people he deigns to associate with. Isn't that right, Papa?"

"So the story goes. I was always pleased to see him, especially thirty-odd years ago." Mr. Stewart turned to his wife. "I saw him here, in this summerhouse, the afternoon before you accepted my offer of marriage."

Mrs. Stewart produced her handkerchief, wiping her eyes. "Silly beggar. I suspect that was this moggy's great-grandfather, but I appreciate the sentiment."

Rex rose, to make an elaborate bow. "I'd like to offer my thanks for being such a wonderful hostess. You've made me welcome in a way none of the other society couples have done, except for the ones who had eligible daughters. They've been positively overwhelming and thus to be avoided at all costs. Too many people try to pussyfoot around me because of this." He tapped his leg. "So I take it as a compliment that you treat me as one of the family."

"You'd do better than most of us, Rex." Jonty pointed to his own leg. "You'd have the advantage of not feeling the smacks."

At supper, the weather was still on the warm side, the wine was cold and the salmon perfection. The conversation in the drawing room was pleasant and the only gloomy note was when Mrs. Stewart left to have a word with the rector's sister, who'd called ostensibly about some charitable matter but probably to get another look at the houseful of young men. The departure of the chatelaine always left an empty feeling which was almost tangible. Not only her benign presence, but her cheer and handsome looks were always missed.

Mr. Stewart, however, recognised these occasions as being excellent ones for discussing sleuthing, something his dear lady wife had frowned upon since the Woodville Ward case, an investigation which she alleged had increased her grey hairs threefold. "Now Jonty, Orlando, are you sure you have the right man?"

"Papa, your perspicacity never ceases to amaze me. We've told you half of nothing about the ins and outs of this case yet you hit the nail right on the head." Jonty stopped, eyed his father with suspicion. "Or have you got a spy?"

Mr. Stewart grinned. "I don't bribe Mrs. Ward to tell tales, if that's what you're thinking. You're not the only one in the family with brains, my lad—I see the rationale of Rhodes killing Jardine, but like you, the whole business with Taylor puzzles me."

"Indeed." Orlando valued his "father-in law's" sensible opinions. "If he did do it, then why? And if he didn't, why say that he did?"

"I don't think that he can be like my pal." Rex swirled his tawny port in its elegant little glass. "From what you told us, Rhodes seemed to be too quick offloading his own sins to pick up everyone else's."

"The only person it would seem he would want to protect is Andrew Nicholls." Mr. Stewart had gained a deep understanding of the case from the snippets he'd picked up, pasting them together to create a clear estimate of the whole. "He seems to be the focus of the man's life."

"Jonty." The name came out slowly and languorously, as it always did when Orlando was either feeling amorous or deep in thought. "When you saw that picture of Nicholls, what did you think?"

"That he looked like a Stewart by-blow—the sort of chap who might have been produced if one of my uncles had gone astray."

"And Kermode? You're the only one of us who's seen him. Was he the same?"

"Along the same lines, although you knew that already. It was part of the rationale of why we were targeted."

Both Rex and Matthew must have registered the word "we" and understood its significance. While it pained Orlando to witness such frankness, it heartened him to hear his beloved be able to so casually refer to such events. The looks exchanged in the garden hadn't lied—Jonty was starting to heal.

"We understand that." Mr. Stewart poured his son a cup of coffee, creamy and sweet, just as he liked it, then passed the cup across. "Although I think I know what Orlando is getting at here. It's very important for us to understand how deep that resemblance went."

"The cat," Rex murmured.

Jonty's eyes reflected the glow of possible enlightenment. He shut them and sipped his drink, as if he were trying to transport himself back to Norfolk. "Simon Kermode looked like a Stewart as well, less like me than he did Andrew Nicholls, though. Sorry, that's not clear. He resembled me, but he resembled Nicholls much more. They might have passed for brothers." He opened his eyes. "Does that help?"

"I think so." Orlando felt like a boy at Christmas, with delights all around. "When I first met Rhodes, we were taking tea with his aunt and she started to talk about having seen a ghost. Her nephew reacted very strangely, immediately terminating the conversation. I assumed it was his unease at the old lady beginning to ramble. People don't feel comfortable in the presence of mental frailty, do they?"

"Indeed not." Matthew seemed to have grasped Orlando's reasoning as well. "You've changed your mind about your interpretation?"

"I have. In fact, afterwards, I did wonder whether he was thinking of his own ghosts, the victims he'd hurt, then I quite forgot the thing, until we met that moggy this afternoon." Orlando couldn't miss the four frowns suddenly on display. "Sorry, that noble cat in the garden. Then I recalled the conversation and it's been nagging at me since then. Now I think I understand."

"Well, I don't." Matthew looked puzzled. "Would you enlighten me?"

"I think we should make him work it out himself." Rex slapped his good leg. "There's enough clues, Matthew. Rhodes's obsession with this poor lad, doppelgangers all round and a cat who might be a ghost or just a plain kitchen mouser."

"We've all suffered enough for this case." Matthew tipped his head to Jonty, who replied with a nod and a smile. "Take pity on me and tell me what everyone's worked out and I haven't." A sly grin crossed his face. "Or else I might have to tell Mrs. Stewart I suspect you've been eating chocolate after you've cleaned your teeth at night. All of you." No male member of the Stewart household or any of their guests was going to risk that sort of threat.

*

"I wonder where Macgregor has put us tonight?" It had become a running joke—the footman had been at his subtle, sensitive best the last few days, taking it into his head to decide at random which bed would be graced with the academic backsides on any given night. He didn't alternate, the only clues would be that the fire in one room had been made up, the hot water bottles (if needed) would be ensconced between the sheets and the pyjamas would be carefully folded, in waiting.

They'd first encountered Macgregor—a man with a Scottish name, Welsh ancestry, and cockney accent—when he'd been a footman and the men had stayed at the Stewarts' London home for the Derby. He'd been assigned to them by Mrs. Stewart, who knew that sensitive matters might be involved. While she said she trusted Jonty not to be in bed with his lover when the morning tea arrived, she couldn't be sure that the untidy little rascal wouldn't leave his shirt on Orlando's floor. He *had* done the latter, of course, and Macgregor hadn't batted an eyelid.

Jonty found that this man of great discretion had, tonight, put them in Orlando's room. He'd also found somewhere a wonderful selection of tulips, which he'd placed in a cut crystal glass on the table and which showed no sign of bending or drooping. This was another thing which Jonty found quite puzzling, as no one else he knew could achieve this. The fire was banked up, as the night was promising to be a bit chilly, and the first feelings of cold were starting to penetrate as he began to strip off.

"Putting your pyjamas on then, Jonty?"

"No, I'm changing into my gumboots and a fur coat. What a ridiculous question."

"Twit." Orlando rolled his eyes and looked pained. "I meant are you putting your nightclothes on or wandering around *au naturel* as per your occasional scandalous practice?"

"Which would you prefer?"

"Doesn't bother me. Never seems to bother you either." Orlando tried hard to hide his excitement.

This was more like his old Jonty, but no chickens were to be counted just yet. "And what do we mean by that, monsieur?"

"That you seem as happy prancing around in your birthday suit as in a three-piece one. Not an inch— if, in the immortal words of Mr. Cartwright, 'you'll excuse the pun'—of bashfulness about you."

"Well, why should I hide my body? There's only you to see it, Orlando, and none of it is unfamiliar." Jonty removed the last of his clothes then leaned against the mantelpiece. Starkers.

"All of it is wonderfully well-known, indeed. And some of it's going to get scorched if you stand there too long. Macgregor has got that fire really blazing—it's going to start spitting cinders in a moment and one of them will end up on your hmphmphm…"

"I never thought I'd ever live to have to shut *you* up with a kiss." Jonty grinned when the sudden embrace ended. "I shall take your very sensible advice. Not an easy place to put a poultice on should *it* get singed and however would I explain the injury to Mama? Come on, get this stuff off." He pulled at Orlando's shirt. "Then we can get over to that bed, out of the danger zone."

"Strikes me," murmured Orlando, as he tried to undo his buttons and be dragged to the four-poster at the same time, "that you might be moving out of danger but I'm moving right into it."

"No danger with me. Make you happy, make you squirm, make you squeal although I'd never hurt you."

"Nor I you." Orlando drew his fingers along his lover's shoulders. "Something's happened, today. Something wonderful, yet I don't know what prompted it."

"If Dr. Coppersmith requires a logical answer I'm afraid he's going to be disappointed. It was an amalgamation of things; Mary Magdalene thinks she's only talking to the gardener, we see the cat which might just be a ghost, and all of a sudden I've got hold of those last two pieces of the puzzle." Jonty doodled on Orlando's chest. "A buzzing in my brain has been nagging me ever since Rhodes confessed. *Job's not done, Jonty. See it to the end.* Had me half scared, not knowing what might be coming next."

"Why didn't you tell me?"

"You'd have rolled your eyes at me, like you always do. *Messages from upstairs*, *again*? Well, perhaps it was—justice needing to be served and all that. And it will be."

"That's just one piece, though, making sure we get the right man for Taylor's murder." Orlando kissed his friend's hair, savoured the lavender odour which, rather than being from a bottle, came from the idiot sticking sprigs of it behind his ears. "What's the other?"

"I've spent years wondering if I contributed to what happened. If there was something I said or did which brought them down on me. Whether if I'd done differently none of it would have happened. As of today, I've realised it was just a chance of my face and features, none of my doing at all. You can't imagine how free that makes me feel." Jonty stretched like the grey cat waiting for his tummy to be tickled.

Orlando obliged, trying to find something, anything, to say which would keep his tears at bay. "Do you remember those books? The ones which Dr. Peters wanted me to destroy, the ones we found in Lord Morcar's rooms?"

"I do, although I never saw them, thank the Lord. Why mention them now?"

"Because they scared the pants off me, or well and truly onto me, I might say. All the time they seemed to equate *this*..."

"Do you mean making love, Orlando?" Jonty gently ran his hand down his lover's neck, onto his chest, found his heart.

"Hmm. Yes. Equated *this* with violence and degradation. I was a right twit, wasn't I?" Orlando smiled, placing his hand over his lover's.

"That's the problem with ignorance, my dear, it isn't necessarily blissful. It breeds fear—you just have to look at my poor sister Lavinia to realise that. I do wonder if Angela Stafford will go the same way."

"Not wishing those ladies any offence, Jonty, but I'm so pleased I didn't end up like that. Glad I found how wonderful things could really be."

"And I'm pleased for it too. Now will you ever doff those trousers or am I to lie here desperate while you talk my head off?"

Perhaps they were more rambling than the average pair of lovers—who knew what went on in another man's bedroom?—but when it was time for bodies to make final communication, they wasted few words. There was no requirement for long-winded protestations of love, vows of eternal fidelity. They knew how much in love they were, all of their life together proclaimed the fact.

After a while, an exquisite, adagio period of slow, sensual kisses and lazy movements of fingers on flesh, Jonty broke free from the knot their bodies had made. The agreeable tangle of arms and legs was picked apart, Jonty marvelling yet again how the familiar could be so exciting. There wasn't an inch of his lover's body he didn't know inside out, and yet every time they became intimate there were new delights to discover. He wondered whether his parents felt the same, if their marital bed still had undiscovered possibilities, and whether that was one of the keys to their long, happy relationship. Richard Stewart swore that keeping a mistress was sinful, yet why would any man even need one if he could be as happy at his own hearth as Jonty was at his?

The music began again, played on the instruments of skin, flesh, mouth and fingers. The fire had grown low, its pale orange light illuminating a pair of bodies rising and falling, the slow rhythm of their amorous duet at first diminuendo, allowing every moment to be savoured at leisure. Mezzo-piano caresses, pianissimo moans, delicate touches and kisses, until the mood changed with, *poco a poco* crescendo, the cadence increasing. A sweet bolero for two dancers together, united as one in time and motion, the escalating tempo matched by mounting exhilaration and anticipation. A handful more drumbeats, strong tympanic strokes and the music was over, duettists spent, tired, blissful. A horizontal symphony, the music of true love.

Chapter Twelve

Dr. Stewart and Sergeant Cohen sat at the table in the prison visitors' room, waiting for Rhodes to be brought. Jonty felt he'd never seen a more depressing place. The Chief Constable of Surrey had been so appalled by the incompetence his officers had shown in the Lord Christopher Jardine investigation, he'd asked Scotland Yard to be brought in and had then insisted *they* draft in the men from Cambridge to see the case to its conclusion.

Or so the sergeant gleefully informed Jonty, *sotto voce*. "And I got the impression the Chief Constable secretly wishes that Mr. Wilson would grow disillusioned with life in Cambridge and move to somewhere like Guildford. It's all highly irregular, of course, but if it means that the right man gets brought to justice…" Cohen shrugged. "This case has been a bit close to home, hasn't it, sir?" An avuncular smile lit up his large, plain face. "Glad to see you looking a lot better now."

"Thank you, Mr. Cohen. Strange as it may seem, I've developed a sort of peace these last few weeks that I never imagined I'd find."

The door opened and Rhodes—escorted by two prison warders—entered and sat down. His guards prepared to stay, but Cohen spoke a word in their ears and, under protest, they left. The prisoner looked tired yet calm. If he was frightened or troubled he gave no sign of it. "Dr. Stewart, we meet again. And this is…?"

"Sergeant Cohen, of the Cambridgeshire Constabulary. He's here at the request of Surrey police."

Rhodes nodded, as if this made entire sense. "Mr. Cohen. May I help you gentlemen?"

"I wish to clarify the matter of Timothy Taylor's death." Jonty fixed his adversary with a piercing blue gaze. "I'm entirely satisfied that you killed Jardine, and I know what motivated you, but I can't say the same of the other death. Did you really murder Taylor?"

"Do you doubt my word so much?"

"You've given me plenty of cause to do so in the past." Jonty's tense fingers drummed on the table. "This time, to my astonishment, I think you've been surprisingly honest. I've looked at Dr. Coppersmith's record of his conversation with you and I'm not surprised at your adherence to the literal truth in what you had to say. It was very clever. But then you always were a very intelligent man."

"And you don't think that I was careful in what I said to you?"

"I've gone over that too—it seems a strange mixture of falsehood and truth. When you spoke of me or Kermode I think you lied, time and again. You were never contrite, Mr. Rhodes, not over us. But when you spoke of Nicholls I think you believed every word, even though I believe you were still far from the reality of things. You were considering Nicholls all the time, making events appear favourable towards him."

"And?" Rhodes seemed as if he'd come to terms with the fact that he was likely to be hanged. No fear or apprehension here, just the effect of someone playing cat and mouse.

"I believe that you were still covering for him when you confessed to killing Taylor. Do you believe in ghosts, Mr. Rhodes?" Jonty remembered the butterflies he'd seen in a museum as a child. Pinned to the card, trapped and preserved forever because of their beauty. Was he pinning his tormentor in his guilt, as the housemaster had tried to capture Nicholls?

The other man turned as pale as the ghosts they were discussing. "I—I beg your pardon?"

"I believe you heard me aright the first time. Do you believe in ghosts? Have you ever seen one?"

"Who told you?" Rhodes's eyes were welling with tears. The sergeant—bluff, bull-like, unexpectedly kind Cohen—handed him a handkerchief.

"You did. You intimated it to my friend Dr. Coppersmith. And when you saw Simon Kermode emerging from Taylor's house you thought it was the ghost of Andrew Nicholls. They really are very alike."

"Kermode? The name seems familiar…"

"It was the other boy, the one they used before me. He had been to see Taylor and you thought it was Nicholls come to take vengeance for all of us. Especially when you found Taylor dead."

"There was blood everywhere. It was like a scene from a biblical painting—the slaughter of the innocents or the striking down of some army in the book of Judges. And I had seen the avenging angel who'd come with his sword to do the deed." Rhodes bore a beatific look again, just like when he'd confessed to the crime.

"It was no angel. Just another one of your victims, armed with a poker and a burden of fury." Jonty felt like an archangel himself, bright with righteous anger. "I don't know why he struck down his abuser at that particular point, although I can guess. But it was Kermode and not Nicholls who did the deed, so you don't need to take the blame for him any more. He was innocent of this."

"Is that true? Was it really this other boy? Not my Andrew?" Rhodes's excitement, his shining eyes and shaking hands, startled his interrogators.

"It is. It was." Jonty had no proof of what he said, not yet, but Orlando believed it, which was good enough.

"Then please tell your superior officers," Rhodes addressed Cohen for the first time, "that I withdraw my confession to the second crime. I will, however, stand by my acknowledgement of the first."

"Might I ask a question at this point?" It seemed odd that the sergeant had to seek permission of Jonty but in the circumstances it felt right for them both.

"Please do. I've ascertained all I need to know." Jonty laid his shaking hands in his lap, felt his heart racing fit to burst. It was done—at last it was all over.

"Mr. Rhodes, you say you found Taylor already dead. Did you check that he wasn't just injured?"

"I had no need to. Did you see his head, Mr. Cohen? There was no earthly way in which he could have survived such an attack."

Cohen nodded—they hadn't seen the body although they'd read the gruesome reports. "Did you notice anything else? If Taylor was dead we're assuming Kermode had already done the deed, but we still need solid evidence to convict him. Can you help us?"

Rhodes nodded. "I found something there. I'll sign a statement to that effect, if you assure me once more that it really was a living man I saw leaving that house. If you go to Epsom you'll find it in the drawer of my desk. Dr. Stewart might recognise it, it's the badge like the one he wore on his blazer as a member of St. Vincent house. I found it next to Taylor's body and I believed Andrew had put it there as a sign of his displeasure. I now see that this other man—what was his name?—must have either left it deliberately or let it fall by accident."

"I'll make sure we find this badge and then I'll return to take your statement." Cohen adopted his most workmanlike tones. There was strong emotion at work all around him and he felt the need to be above it all.

"And Mr. Cohen," Rhodes said softly, eyes streaming with tears, "would you please check that my aunt is coping? I do worry about her."

Orlando made an appointment to see Kermode at his shop, ostensibly to look at some wonderfully obscure mathematical works from the late eighteenth century. He took Inspector Wilson with him, not simply in case an arrest was necessary but as a form of protection. He'd seen one murderer cornered before and knew how dangerous they could become.

They kept up a degree of subterfuge, Orlando being so interested in the dusty old tomes he purchased one of them, Wilson all the while hovering in the background looking at sailing prints. At the appropriate moment Orlando murmured a few words to Kermode concerning Dr. Stewart, the recent murders, the true identity of the man interested in the etching of HMS Victory and the need to gain a little help in securing Rhodes's conviction. Kermode sent his assistant out for a lengthy lunch then focussed his attention on the two men.

"We are very grateful," Wilson began, "for the information you gave Dr. Stewart. Your help ultimately led us to identify Sebastian Rhodes as the man who killed Jardine."

"You're sure he was the killer?" Kermode looked pale, concerned.

"We are. We have the man's confession, although we still need to establish the facts in case he changes his plea in court. Men do." The smell of books, dusty, age-worn, seemed to stifle the air in the room, suspend all life within it for a few moments.

"It is odd how this case revolved around *those three*." Kermode looked at his hands. "How every thread seemed to be linked to St. Vincent house."

"That seems to me inevitable." Orlando spoke slowly and carefully. "Once Jardine decided to make a form of public confession, then all those who had been touched by this case—perpetrators and victims— would be dragged in."

"How can I help further? I gave a full statement to the local police about my visit to Dorking."

"And very clear and helpful it was, sir." Wilson spoke the truth. All agreed it had been a cogent and sensible explanation. "But we'd like to know if you can give us any help regarding the second crime to which Rhodes has confessed."

"Which crime is that?"

"The murder of Timothy Taylor." Orlando and the inspector hadn't planned in advance who would ask what. After the experience in Epsom with Jonty changing the script, Orlando was wary of doing it anyway. But this was a question *he* had to pose—he was Jonty's champion, not Wilson. "A man who resembled you was seen going into Taylor's house the morning he was killed. We wondered if you'd been to visit him."

"This man resembled me, you say? Well, I don't have any particular outstanding attributes, it might have been anyone. Even your friend Dr. Stewart. I know from the evidence of my own eyes that we're alike."

"There is a certain similarity." The words stuck in Orlando's craw. "Although there's someone else to whom you bear a stronger resemblance. Mr. Wilson?"

The inspector produced the picture which had graced Rhodes's desk and gave it to Kermode. The man might have been looking at a photograph of his brother.

"Who is this?" Kermode's hand trembled.

"A boy called Andrew Nicholls. He was the one who died in mysterious circumstances, an accident that may well have been suicide, prior to your time at school."

Wilson was studying Kermode's face. Orlando had seen that penetrative look before—it was like a mongoose with a snake under its spell. "You see, we have a witness who thought they saw Nicholls going into Taylor's house. That can't be possible, so we need to find someone who looks similar enough to be mistaken for him. Dr. Stewart bears a passing likeness, but not enough to convince, and anyway he was attending church with several members of the royal family so is to be counted out entirely."

"Then so am I, I'm afraid. I was at mass—Brompton Oratory, you know." Kermode must have been trying his best to look suitably pious. "With Mama."

"Really? I know that your mother was in attendance, and that she was accompanied by a young man who was very conscientious in his attentions to her." The inspector leaned forwards. "Whether that man was actually you, I have my doubts."

Kermode paled. "Why should I want to visit Taylor? I had nothing to say to him. He hadn't felt a moment's remorse about what he did, not like Jardine. I've not even seen him since those days at school."

Wilson reached into his pocket, producing a small packet which he carefully and elaborately unwrapped. "Mr. Kermode, do you recognise this?" He tipped out a bright metal object which had made a careful journey (with Mr. Cohen in the Stewarts' coach) from Epsom Downs to London, thence by train to Cambridge and Wilson's eager hand.

Kermode reached for the little badge which lay revealed, but was restrained from touching the bright metal. "It's a house badge, from my old school."

"As you say, everything keeps coming back to St. Vincent house." Orlando regarded the other man steadily. If Kermode recognised the little emblem as his own he gave no sign. "Might this be yours?"

"No." The answer came a little too quickly. "I don't know where mine is. Think I threw it away when I left that ghastly place."

"This was found next to Taylor's body. It must have been placed there, or dropped accidentally, perhaps by an old pupil, or someone from their close family. I did wonder whether your mother had taken it with her as some sort of a talisman when she stove Taylor's head in." Orlando noticed the anger flaring in Kermode's eye and was pleased to see it. A rattled man might say all sorts of things he didn't intend to.

"How dare you accuse my mother—"

"We're not accusing her." Wilson turned the badge in his fingers. Dazzling shafts of light reflected and danced from it, producing an almost hypnotic effect. "We know that she was at the Oratory. She was seen by several people who could vouch for her and whose word I accept. You, however, were not known to these witnesses and I only have your mother's word to them that the man she introduced was her son. Resemblance again—it seems to saturate this case."

"Mr. Kermode." Orlando was becoming frustrated, seeing no sensible way through this man's veneer. "It would be easy to arrange for the witness who saw you entering Taylor's house to be asked to positively identify you. Likewise those who vouched for you at mass could be asked to review their conviction in the light of seeing you in person."

"Then do that, Dr. Coppersmith, I have nothing to fear."

"Don't you? No fear at all? That amazes me." Orlando had a plan beginning to form in his mind. It wasn't particularly fair, yet it might prove effective. "My dear friend Dr. Stewart suffered as you did at the hands of these men, and he's told me often of the fears and unhappiness he was left with. Are you saying that you haven't been affected as he is?"

Kermode blanched, studied his hands. "I'm not saying that at all. If you have any idea of what Dr. Stewart truly endured then you'll know the nightmares I've had. But those who people my dreams are now either dead or in prison facing a capital sentence. I don't believe that I've anything further to fear."

The man's face contradicted his words—Orlando ploughed on. "Something Dr. Stewart found odd was how his demons weren't quite as he'd built them up to be in his imagination. Jardine had repented, unexpectedly but genuinely. Rhodes is a loving nephew who shows a real devotion to his aunt." Words stuck again in Orlando's throat but he was learning how to dissemble. "Did you find the same?"

Kermode looked puzzled. "I haven't seen Sebastian Rhodes since I left school, but Jardine was much changed, you're right. He was less arrogant, less sure of himself, less angry, I suppose you might say."

"Perhaps that was because of his remorse." Orlando tried hard to seem like he was just woolgathering. "He wasn't unwell, perchance? Intimations of his own mortality making him want to confess all?"

Kermode snorted. "No, he was as hale and hearty as any of us. He hadn't started to show signs of the sins of the flesh, like his partner in crime."

"Dr. Stewart was certainly surprised at the deterioration in Taylor's condition—we speculated long and hard as to its cause. What do you think? TB or something more sinister?"

"It looked like the pox of some sort to me, Dr. Coppersmith." Kermode began to laugh. "Served the bastard right."

"I suspect that cough might have made it hard for the man to survive another winter, not a healthy sound at all." A tiny smile graced Orlando's face. "Mr. Kermode, I'd say it wasn't a healthy sound. Don't you agree?"

"You bastard. You absolute swine." Kermode rose, aimed a futile blow at Orlando, but the man was too quick for him. He was used to avoiding Jonty's swipes. "You tricked me. Lulled me into saying things I shouldn't have done."

"That's enough of that." Wilson grasped Kermode's arm firmly as Orlando carried on, undaunted. "You said you hadn't seen Taylor since school days. The only way you could know how he'd changed would be the evidence of your own eyes and ears."

Kermode reached for one of the books on his desk, as if he might launch it at his interrogators. Instead, he caressed the leather binding, regaining his composure. "Have you considered that I might have heard about the change in Taylor's condition from someone else? Perhaps your *friend* Dr. Stewart?"

"I know that you didn't hear it from him, so who could have told you? Jardine, I suppose? At least we could verify that fact, as Rhodes seems to have overheard your entire conversation the night he was killed." Orlando was next to Kermode now, his chair edged so close that they almost touched. "Don't lie to me. I wonder if you wore gloves when you went to see Taylor? Mr. Wilson's colleagues have an array of fingerprints from his home and they'll be very interested to see if any of yours match. Nice corroborative evidence, once we take into account the statement of the man who impersonated you at church." It was a lie, a huge lie, but Orlando was beyond caring. He wanted the truth, for Jonty's sake, the absolute and awful truth.

Kermode could hardly speak. "How did you know? How did you find him?" He sat down, head in hands.

Orlando noted the dark look Wilson gave him, no doubt surprised at the tactics employed. Was the inspector sympathetic? Had he ever bent the truth himself and would he know how effective it could be as a strategy? It seemed to have worked now. "Are you now admitting that you weren't at mass?"

"Of course. There's no point lying if you have Robin Gray's word for things. He did a good job, but I should have guessed our luck couldn't hold." Kermode sat up straight, suddenly businesslike. "I went to see Taylor and I ended up killing him, making it look similar to the way Jardine had died. I never thought I'd say that I found a newspaper useful, but that particular report stuck in my mind. I didn't set out to kill him, you must believe me—it was when I heard him refusing to take responsibility for what he did at school, and making fun of Jardine because the man had a change of heart, I could bear it no longer. I punched him, he fell down and I finished him off with the poker." He might have been doing nothing more than discussing an old manuscript.

"Why set up an alibi if you didn't go with murder in mind?" Wilson spoke before Orlando could. He felt the need to take control of the interview back into official hands, before a third murder got committed.

"Because I didn't want to be caught up with these men at all. There had been one killing and I knew I might be considered a suspect for it, having been there on the night. I had to cover my tracks this time, Mama was insistent." Kermode drew out a handkerchief, passed it over his face. "I would have spared Taylor, you know, if he'd shown the slightest bit of remorse. If he'd used the simple word *sorry* he would still be alive."

There was silence. The smell of the books seemed musty and unpleasant now, not evocative of well- kept libraries but of houses gone to ruin. The reflections from the little badge, still in Wilson's hand, seemed sharp and cruel, fixing the eye and holding it. The case was over, leaving a bitter taste for everyone. Guilt and innocence, repentance and forgiveness, they twisted, tangled and made little sense.

Chapter Thirteen

From *The Times* of April 30th, 1907:
Today at the Old Bailey: Mr. Sebastian Henry Rhodes of Old Oaks, Epsom, Surrey, pleaded guilty to the murder of Lord Christopher Jardine. This appalling crime took place on 1st February, 1907; the accused had been said to hold a personal grudge against the deceased. Sentencing has been delayed while the judge listens to medical reports.

It seemed for a while that Rhodes was going to evade the noose, his solicitor pleading that no sane man could make a false confession to a murder just because he believed in ghosts. The testimony of a leading psychiatrist and the evidence of conversations where the accused was very clearly endeavouring to hide his guilt—making rational and complex mental leaps—swung the balance in the judge's mind, making a capital sentence inevitable.

Jonty insisted that he and Orlando spend the day either side of the execution at his parents' home. They didn't celebrate, all of them recognised that would have been wrong, but they shared the sense of relief that an unpleasant episode could be put behind them. Mrs. Stewart cried again, Orlando offered his handkerchief, she kissed his cheek fondly and called him son, so even in the most difficult of times, a ray of hope shone.

From a letter dated May 4th, the same year:
I would like to thank you, again, for the efforts you showed on my behalf. I believe Mr. Collingwood would have sorted things in the end, although your endeavours no doubt brought things to an earlier conclusion. My sister says that you were diligent in your hard work and also very charming to her. I'll take her word for it. I apologise again that I haven't been to offer my thanks personally, but I have been very busy trying to pick up the reins of my life once more. There has been a lot of talk of "no smoke without fire" and I fear that I'll have to resort to moving abroad to free myself of people's prejudices. I have even found this coldness among those I would call my friends.

The letter droned on with more of the same, Alistair Stafford bearing more than one chip on his shoulder and aiming several of his barbs at Matthew Ainslie. Orlando thought the whole thing ungentlemanly, lacking in proper gratitude to the people who'd risked so much to help him.

Jonty simply wondered what Matthew had ever seen in the man and, with a snort, suggested that perhaps the continent was the best place for him. Hopefully he'd meet up with Robbie Ross or, better still, Alfred Douglas, and they could all be miserable together.

From *The Times* of May 12th:
Today at the Old Bailey, the trial began of Simon Kermode for the murder of Timothy Taylor on 10th March last. Mr. D Ballantine defending. The prosecution allege that Kermode committed the crime in revenge for gross acts which had been committed by the deceased when they were boys at school. They said that the crown would produce witnesses who had seen the accused in the area of the victim's house at the time concerned and others who would swear that the alibi he had given police was a false one.

Kermode was found guilty, weighed down by circumstantial evidence, not least from the man who'd been persuaded to impersonate him at mass to secure his alibi. The wholly damning fingerprint found at the scene, and later identified as Kermode's, had whitewashed over the tears and pleas from his mother.

Jonty had been impassive about it all, showing sympathy for the accused yet still not wanting to defend him. After all, he'd suffered similarly and not once taken the law into his hands, no matter how great the temptation had been.

From a letter dated May 17th, from Mrs. Stewart to her youngest child:
Jonty, your father and I would be delighted to accept your invitation to spend some time at Forsythia Cottage as long as it won't impose on Mrs. Ward. It must be bad enough having you two to look after, the poor woman surely has her work cut out all the time. Richard will be delighted to see the May bumps again. I'll warrant we'll have to tie him to a convenient lamppost to stop him trying to find a boat that would have him. You know he would love to have the chance to win an oar.

We are so pleased that all this business has now come to an end with that poor lad Kermode being found guilty. You were both magnificent in the witness box; we were most proud of you. I did confer with Richard at the time about whether it wouldn't have been better to let Rhodes take the blame for both cases, but your father always knows best. "The truth must be served, Helena, whether it leads to pain or gain." It seems such a shame that a poor benighted lad, who had suffered as you did and was only taking the sort of revenge that any of us might have, ended up with being hung. Sometimes I think that the system of English justice is all wrong.

I hope that you're both wearing your vests on the chillier nights as I don't want you catching cold. I suppose that you have each other to keep you warm but that is not the point.

"Dearest Mama," Jonty remarked, blowing his nose to cover up his emotion.

Orlando smiled and squeezed his lover's hand.

Jonty acted peculiarly in the run-up to his parents' arrival, making strange noises along the lines of "don't think we should share a bed while the old folk are here" despite the fact they'd done so while being the Stewarts' guests. Orlando understood and they slept apart all the time, much to the unspoken amusement of the other people in the house.

The bumps were magnificent, the Bride's boat finishing them as Head of the River and everyone bar Mrs. Stewart ending up tired, emotional and needing a long pre-prandial nap.

Extract of a letter dated June 1st, from Mrs. Ward to her son:
I find it hard to believe that I've been here nearly half a year. My academical men, as you call them, are proving very easy to look after; all one has to provide are endless quantities of cake and they're happy, just like you when you were seven. I sometimes think of them as being nothing but boys, all muddy trousers and scuffed boots, then I see them reading one of their books and I remember that they're very clever men, highly respected not just within the University but, so I hear, across the country.

Dr. Stewart had his parents here to stay. His father has a title, you know, yet doesn't choose to use it, which astonished me, but when I met him I wasn't at all surprised—not an air or grace between them. Mrs. Stewart would help me with the chores whenever I condescended to let her. I rather think she's annoyed that she missed out on being the sort of mother who's allowed to cook, mend and clean up after her brood. Isn't that strange, when you consider how many hardworking mothers would gladly swap places with her? They live in a castle and I'm to visit them in the summer when my gentlemen travel there. Imagine that, your mother living in a castle. (Although I do hope it's below stairs, I couldn't take the embarrassment of being a guest of the family).

To answer your question, yes, my gentlemen are the ones who do the detecting, like Mr. Holmes. And very successful they are—the police seem to always be here consulting them. I was even allowed to help a little in their last case, so you will be astounded to know that your mother was material in catching a murderer.

I hope that you are wearing your thickest clothes…

July 2nd, a quiet private beach on the coast of Massachusetts.

Two men lying on the white sands, tired from swimming out to the rocks, surfeited with salad and champagne. Rex Prefontaine resting on his elbow, taking handfuls of fine sand, letting it drizzle through his fist and pile up on Matthew Ainslie's strong chest. They'd swum, sported on the rocks, come to rest on the soft clean sands and were drinking in the pleasures of the strand with great delight. It had amazed Matthew that Rex's artificial limb made not a scrap of difference to either his mobility or his zest for life—they'd run and climbed like two small lads.

The time had come now to put away childish things—they were both too strongly aware of each other's masculinity to delay the inevitable much longer. From almost the first time they'd met, in that train carriage full of surprises, the exchange of looks, gestures, banter had sent out clear signals of mutual attraction.

In deference to their hostess they'd banned not just talk of business but of anything else, yet it had been alluded to. The intensity of their attraction, the sheer exhilaration pictured on their faces, made their outward appearance even more striking than it already was. If there had been parasols in the area they would have been twirled provocatively, hankies would have been dropped, sighs would have been made very audible. On this beach the men were alone and it was just as well.

They made a handsome couple, lying out on the sand, muscles scarcely contained by their bathing suits—an ornament to any gathering, a fine pair of men.

"I hate the beach if there are women about. I always suspect them of fantasising about me," Rex confessed as they soaked up the sun. "Don't look so shocked, I'm not that vain. Some of the more forward Massachusetts minxes tell me so."

"And what do you say to them?"

"That I've never dreamed of anything but cash registers or the raising of Aberdeen Angus cattle." Rex smiled, sighed, drizzled more sand onto Matthew's chest. "I like women, although only the hearty, maternal type, not young, flirty ones. And then just as pleasant company. For anything else I prefer a man—one who's quiet, intelligent, sensible and amusing."

Matthew guessed the words were aimed at him but knew they'd apply equally well to his host. Alistair Stafford was now free, somewhere on the continent or so rumour had it, still bitter, resentful, conceited, handsome, childish. He could stay there, out of Matthew's life forever. "Will we go out again tonight for a walk under the moon? I've never heard such a cacophony of insect noise."

"If you wish. All the business is pretty well sealed, there's nothing else on that front until the papers come back from the legal men and we see how they want to poke their noses in. Under the moon it is, but..." Rex stopped drizzling sand, looked serious. "Look—this publishing business isn't the only merger I have in mind, if you get my drift."

"I think—" Ainslie swallowed hard, containing the excitement, "—I catch it entirely."

"Then tonight, you let me kiss you, okay?" Rex grinned broadly, ridiculously handsome and full of life under the blazing sun.

"Aw, Rex." Ainslie produced an approximation of the East Coast drawl. "Why wait till tonight?"

July 2nd. Delivery of a package to Forsythia Cottage, around breakfast time. "Don't you like it then?"

"It's very well made, but then I'd expect that of Waite's." Orlando sounded as if he'd made purchases at those particular tailors all his life.

"You still haven't answered the question."

"It's very nice. I'm just not sure that red velvet is really my sort of thing, in a jacket. When would I wear it?"

"High Table, naturally. Oh steady on, don't choke, that was just a joke, you know. You could wear it at Mama's at any time. It would quite turn the old girl's head. But mainly I'd like you to wear it here, at home. For me." Jonty smiled and gently stroked the fabric. He'd ordered the garment secretly, knowing that Waite's had his lover's measurements and would be able to produce a work of art without the sitter being actually present. He had been *with child* to see the finished product. "Put it on for me, please?"

Orlando pulled on the jacket. It fitted to perfection and looked in many ways sensational. It certainly evinced a certain look in both their eyes which made them wish it wasn't breakfast but supper time instead. "Does it make me look like a Nancy boy?"

"No. A hint of the aesthete, although you're far too masculine to worry about that."

"Just as well." Neither man appreciated effeminacy. They were first and foremost men and didn't ever choose to be like women, even if some of their inclination did. "I'll wear it tonight at dinner, which will be here and not at High Table, thank goodness." Orlando smiled. "I don't recommend that you buy one like this. With your slovenly eating habits poor Mrs. Ward would be beside herself trying to keep it clean."

Jonty cocked his head to one side and smiled—it was the look that meant mischief. "We could ask Mrs. Ward to make us a picnic, take it and a bottle of bubbly down to the river. I'll get a punt organised and we can meander along until we find a convenient willow. You can have control of the pole, you like that." He tried an encouraging look and was pleased to see it returned.

"That would be pleasant enough. Long time since we went punting."

"I always thought you were avoiding it, given what happened last time."

Orlando began to redden. "Hmm. Well, that might not be possible this time, given how late it stays light. Bit further on in the year is a much more tempting time."

"Tonight it is, though, Orlando. You can wear that new jacket and I'll count the number of girls who blush or flutter their eyelashes at you. We can stay out very late, stagger home up the Madingley Road and let our good lady housekeeper tell us off." Jonty looked into his lover's eyes and knew that the man couldn't say no.

The evening was perfect, hardly a cloud in the sky to spoil the vast expanse of blue which enveloped Cambridge like the canopy of a great tent. The sun had seemed reluctant to head for the horizon and lingered in the west, colouring the blue with ever-deepening red and orange hues. Perhaps it was determined to treat East Anglia like the Scottish Isles and barely allow a hint of darkness to spoil the evening.

They punted leisurely up the river, finding a sward of green upon which they could spread a rug and enjoy a cold omelette bursting with herbs, some excellent canapés, cake, and more champagne than any man might dare to consume while remaining relatively sober. Jonty wondered whether the police would be likely to come and see if Orlando could steer his punt in a straight line after two glasses of bubbly, which was countered with speculation about whether Jonty would like the punt pole inserted into a certain part of his anatomy.

The punt rested under the willows, peaceful under the darkening sky. It reminded Orlando of sitting beneath the apple tree in the garden of his family home, fascinated by the dappled light through the branches which made strange, flowing patterns on the pages of his books. Trigonometry, they usually concerned, the beautiful interactions of sine and cosine that made sense of line and angle and the ninety- degree corner that had no place in nature. Now he had something, or someone, more beautiful to consider. It was wonderful here, an almost sacred place for them and one where the chances of being caught—while not nonexistent—were very small.

They lay quietly as the gloaming descended, watching the diminution of the light through the curtain of the willow fronds. They chatted, in voices hardly above a murmur, held hands and made plans for the summer ahead. The magnificent red jacket, which had, according to Jonty's tally, turned the heads of fifteen ladies—four of whom were old enough to know better—had been turned on itself and folded to make a silken pillow for their heads, alongside Jonty's older, favourite sports jacket.

"Been an interesting year, hasn't it?" Jonty reached for one of the fronds that canopied them, caressing the long leaves and enjoying the feeling of them going through his fingers.

"Interesting is one word for it. Somehow a quiet existence continues to elude us, and we cram as much excitement into six months as most folk manage in a lifetime." Orlando bravely kissed his lover's brow. "There's been times this year when I was so worried about you, that you might crumble completely under the pressure of turning the chase on Rhodes and his hounds, but you've proved as strong as the very walls of St. Bride's itself. The child of your parents indeed."

Jonty returned Orlando's kiss, not confining himself to forehead but venturing to his cheek. "I suspect *interesting* is the price we pay for wanting to be Sergeant Cuff. You will note that I didn't mention the denizens of Baker Street this time, as I know you object to them."

"You're no doubt right." Orlando parted the green curtains, looking up and down stream, not that much could be seen in the twilight. It would soon be pitch dark, with only the stars to light their way as they eventually punted downstream to stagger home. But they were still young, as madly in love as they'd been eighteen months before and none of this seemed in any way important.

A small but particularly persistent set of fingers made their way across Orlando's stomach and began to insinuate themselves between the buttons of the man's shirt. "No one's going to come along now. Even if they did, they wouldn't notice if we were entirely silent. Entirely." It was as well that Orlando couldn't see the look on his lover's face.

"I can manage that admirably well. I can't vouch for you, though."

"I can be as quiet as a church mouse should I need to be."

"That's not exactly an appropriate analogy, but it will have to do, I suppose." They kissed, began to caress in earnest. "Jonty?"

"Hmm?"

"Do you ever worry that we'll be caught? Knowing this is illegal even when we do it in the privacy of our own home?"

"Well, we're not going to go all the way, are we? It'll overturn the punt for one thing. I think we'd better confine it to relatively innocent activity tonight, especially as we don't want the wrath of Mrs. Ward for soaking that nice new jacket. Although we're actually much further away from any living thing than when we're at home, or when we were in Bride's, so..." The fingers edged on, closer to their intended target, the one which made Orlando roar like a lion.

"It's still illegal."

"I know. And it's a crying bloody shame."

Orlando held his lover closer, although he didn't restrain the wandering hands. "No crying now, Jonty. No more tears."

"I think," Jonty sighed, letting his nomadic hands meander further south, "you could just be right. No need for tears now. All better."

About the Author

Charlie Cochrane's ideal day would be a morning walking along a beach, an afternoon spent watching rugby, and a church service in the evening, with her husband and daughters tagging along, naturally. She loves reading, theatre, good food and watching sport, especially rugby. She started writing relatively late in life but draws on all the experiences she's hoarded up to try to give a depth and richness to her stories.

To learn more about Charlie Cochrane, please visit her website www.charliecochrane.co.uk. You can send an email to Charlie at cochrane.charlie2@googlemail.com or join in the fun with other readers and writers of gay historical romance at **http://groups.yahoo.com/group/SpeakItsName**.